CLAIMING THEIR VILLAGE BRIDE

Claiming Their Bride, Book Two

ABBY AARON

Published by Blushing Books
An Imprint of
ABCD Graphics and Design, Inc.
A Virginia Corporation
977 Seminole Trail #233
Charlottesville, VA 22901

©2019
All rights reserved.

No part of the book may be reproduced or transmitted in any form or by any means, electronic or mechanical, including photocopying, recording, or by any information storage and retrieval system, without permission in writing from the publisher. The trademark Blushing Books is pending in the US Patent and Trademark Office.

Abby Aaron
Claiming Their Village Bride

EBook ISBN: 978-1-948140-58-4
Print ISBN: 978-1-948140-66-9

v1

Cover Art by ABCD Graphics & Design
This book contains fantasy themes appropriate for mature readers only. Nothing in this book should be interpreted as Blushing Books' or the author's advocating any non-consensual sexual activity.

Contents

Prologue	1
1. Wild and Free	7
2. Aras: Bound but Resolved	18
3. Loinbard: Defiantly Free	27
4. Anders: Freed Without a Voice	35
5. Proclaiming their Desire	47
6. Breaking Bread	58
7. Views on Scolding	66
8. Jemina's Challenge	74
9. Lasting Promise	84
10. Gaining a Sister	94
11. Leodon's Challenge	101
12. Smiley's Devotion	108
13. Another Price to be Paid	119
14. Back on Track	126
15. Darnish's Challenge	134
16. Protecting the Fragile	143
17. Narrowing the field of competition	151
18. Ellias' Challenge	161
19. The Claiming	171
20. Truth and Justice for All	181
21. Retrieving their Wayward Wife	193
22. Dreams Come to Pass	203
Abby Aaron	213
Blushing Books	215

To Sandra, a dyslexic's saving grace.

Prologue

Facing Her Penalty

"Stop delaying," her husband, the serious one, demanded. "*Explain why you chose to dishonor our family and dared to convince others to help you?*"

A skilled warrior would cringe under the livid expression he was giving her. But she still did not fear whatever outcome awaited her. Jemina's husbands would never truly harm her, not in a lasting manner. They had sworn to protect her, not once, but twice. Mere hours before, they accepted the cruel punishment meted out by the village elders for her sin of breaking their laws. They shielded her from hard, red-hot rod strikes across the back.

"I had to tell my brother. He needs to protect his wife."

Her amber-haired mate challenged her feeble excuse. "Giannis is under no immediate danger, wife. If she is with child, it would take months for the real threat to come to pass. You are more intelligent than most. Do not try to claim you don't understand as much."

Both men circled around her, and shame coursed through Jemina. She trusted her motives were pure. "I did not realize you three would pay the price for my actions. All I could think of when I left—"

"You agreed to let us handle the task," her third husband interrupted her.

"Do you deny remembering our promise to return to your village and share the secret with Jael?"

"Bride, our family has protected the confidence we shared with you for many cycles. Our sister's life depends on guarding it until she comes of age. After such a time, everyone will know of the city's deceit. No one outside of our immediate family unit can know the full story. Not even Otto, who is trusted more than any other living being among us.

"Yet we did not hesitate to expose the details to you and, in consideration of your wishes as our wife, we promised to extend this knowledge to your brother. Do you comprehend the courage such a compromise cost my blood brother and me? Despite him living far away from our family unit, knowing one slip of his tongue could jeopardize all which we have worked so hard to protect, we agreed to your request to prepare Jael to protect his wife."

"How can I make this right?" Jemina was desperate now. She longed to go back in time and undo the damage to her husbands' trust and respect for her. Whatever they asked of her, she would do it to prove how repentant she was for disrespecting their faith.

"We have gifted you with all we have to offer, Jemina. Our protection. Our love. Our seed." Her first husband's voice sounded so dejected. "You will have to find a way to repair the harm done."

"I cannot undo the damage. The wounds on your backs will remind me always of the day I dishonored our union and selfishly acted alone, instead of putting our family's interest above all others. Jael and my family unit back in Urijah were my primary focus, but I forgot, as your wife, I have a new family unit that rightfully surpasses all others."

She removed her shirt and pants, tossing them aside. Her undergarments followed. She needed to bare herself, body and soul now to prove her honest, pure shame. Her three husbands watched her closely, but she did not meet their eyes. Until she had regained their respect, proven her own, she would not do so. "You have gifted me with your protection. Each of your backs confirm your devotion. The fact that you have not cast me off as a wife, even after I dishonored our family unit, proves your love knows no bounds."

The village bride dropped to her knees and prepared to do the one thing she had managed to avoid during their many lovemaking sessions since the wedding ceremony.

Reaching up, she slowly unfastened her second husband's pants and reached inside. His male member was easy to free. It was already engorged. Shutting her eyes tightly, she promised herself she could find the courage to do this. "Until I earn the right to receive your seed in my womb, I will accept it this way as proof of my regret for leaving the safety of the village border."

The smell was not unpleasant. It reminded her of his strength and devotion to her. Often this husband had explored her body with his mouth, especially her most intimate parts. He was skilled with flicking his hot tongue across her nub, making it swell and go damp. He was even teaching her other husbands about the ways to drive her wild with the same attention.

Could the tip of her tongue move as expertly as his did? She allowed herself to study the end. A small amount of liquid seeped from the slit there. She could not stop herself from gagging at the thought of something so unfamiliar going into her mouth.

Jemina refused to give up. Her husbands loved her above all others. The dew had a musty flavor, she noted as she ran her tongue over the tip. Her husband tensed and a moan tore from deep in his chest.

He was enjoying her efforts. Pride swelled within her heart. He pulled back, moaning about being too close to losing his seed.

She switched attention to her first husband. His member was even harder than the second's had been. With pride and determination, she repeated her earlier action. First, she licked the impressive length. He tasted a bit stronger than the other, but she found herself getting used to the strange sensation and wondered what her third mate would feel and taste like when she was ready to work on him.

Her tongue settled over the tip of her first mate's rod, but she opted to go slower this time. Rushing the act with her second husband had been a miscalculation. "Oh, dear Creator above, this cannot be right." His words were husky, and her first husband held on tightly to her hair as she sucked on the moisture escaping from the tip.

"I have regained my control," her auburn-haired mate announced, coming forward to try coaxing her attention back to him. She switched between both men, licking the very edge around the tips of their shafts before suckling the liquid that rewarded her efforts.

Her third husband pushed his way toward her suddenly. She witnessed him strong arm his triad aside as he freed his own penis. He guided it toward her face, the look of anticipation making Jemina's own body grow damp. She reached down to start fondling herself, but he ordered her to stop.

"You do not come until each of us do," he ordered. His bold words and stern expression almost made her explode. The pungent scent he produced thrilled her.

Fisting her hair, he waited until she parted her teeth more before pushing himself deeper inside. Was she meant to let him take her in the mouth as he did in her channel? Was such a thing even possible? Jemina did gag then, but only for a moment.

He gave her a chance to recover, before beginning to ease in and out of her mouth again, shallow at first, but gaining deeper and deeper access with each thrust. Her hands reached up to brace against his thighs, as if she could try gaining a bit of control over his relentless prodding.

Something wanton inside her took control. She reached up to pull his pants down completely, caressing his balls. Wild, exciting sounds erupted from husband number three. Jemina forced her mouth to go slack and grabbed onto his firm ass, digging her fingers in the taut muscles there. It was not long before he was tensing.

Jemina started using her tongue to playfully push his member out as he pulled back, before dutifully sucking it back inside. If her mouth was not full, she would no doubt be moaning with desire. Hot fluid shot in her throat, and for a moment she was unsure of how to proceed. Her mother had not given her any clues on what to do when pleasing a man this way. Was she meant to swallow as he spilled his seed or let it pool in the back of her mouth until he finished?

"Open your mouth," her third husband commanded, as he pulled himself

free. "I want to see my seed filling your hot mouth before you accept every bit of it when you swallow." At his nod of approval, Jemina sat on her haunches and allowed the seed to slide down her throat, even licking her lips as if appreciative of the gift he bestowed on her.

A huge smile returned to his lips. His anger and disappointment had vanished. "Be warned. If you blatantly disobey us again, it won't be your mouth which claims our seed, but your beautiful, tight ass."

"You would beat me?" she asked in a sassy tone, relieved at least this husband had forgiven her.

"Not beat, little gem. Fuck. We will take turns pumping our cocks into your tight ass."

The image he planted in her mind both terrified and intrigued her.

She started concentrating on her first husband, bringing him close to spilling his seed, but stopped short of finishing him off. With a wicked grin, she turned to the second, taking him to the very edge again, only to pull away.

Then she pulled at each man's legs, drawing them to stand closer to her. Then Jemina guided both men inside her mouth. She could not take either in very deep. Jemina used the side of her mouth as a holding place for one member, as she accepted the other's hard, powerful thrust. Then her face shifted and the other member gained full access while she pocketed the other between her teeth and jaw.

Both came with a force that sent a shudder through all three of their bodies. The volume of seed was hard to contain, and some seeped between her lips as she was freed. She took a moment to regain her composure

They carried her to the bed. They used their mouths and fingers to bring her to completion. For a moment, Jemina actually feared she had accidently relieved herself as her body shuddered out of control. Liquid came shooting out of her frame. Would her husbands notice? She clamped her legs together tightly, only to have them forced apart by strong hands.

To her horror, her auburn hair husband used his mouth to accept the fluid. Then the other two reached over to pry her legs open wider so they could lick away any remaining specks. Her first husband sat beside her, pulling her head to rest on his lap. "Later tonight, we will pour our seed inside your perfect body again. Only this time, we will have two entrances to fill, wife."

DAYBREAK ON NEW EARTH, Village of Urijah

"WAKE UP, girl. The sun is rising. If we hope to complete our journey, we must make haste. It will take two days to travel to both villages and the two sections of the city wall not protected by Urijah warriors.

Jemina's eyes blinked open. Why had he interrupted her wonderful dream? "I will be up in a moment, Papa." Pulling her bed sheets over her chin, she prayed he would leave quickly. She did not know which to be more embarrassed about – having one of her fathers wake her from one of her many wanton dreams or knowing a large pool of her release no doubt spotted her sheets. Would she be able to change the bed before it was time to depart?

Jemina was puzzled about her sleeping thoughts. How could a virgin have such vivid dreams of things she knew nothing about? Only fleeting memories of the actual events in the fantasy lingered as she allowed her fleeting climax to wane. No matter, soon she would learn how accurate her unconscious notions about what it would be like to make love were true. Today she started her journey into a new, exciting life.

Her fathers were finally ready to announce her coming of age. They had put off the task well beyond the general milestone of seventeen cycles. She was nineteen cycles now, soon to be twenty. Jemina would not be held back any longer. She threatened to travel alone and make the announcement herself if her fathers did not do their duty by the end of the official village cycle. With their approval or not, triads of fit warriors would soon compete for the right to wed her. Life as a village born woman was blessed, indeed.

1

Wild and Free

As the heavily cloaked, slender figure rushed ahead of the group yet again, Leodon exhaled with frustration; the profound lines across his weathered brow deepened. "I knew it was a mistake to bring her. We will be lucky to return to our village alive." The dense foliage made it challenging to keep track of the impulsive youth up ahead.

Ellias clapped his heavy palm against his fellow triad member's back. No lines marred his attractive face, and only a touch of gray hinted to his middle age. "Calm yourself, friend. She is safe. Between the three of us, we can handle any mischief which comes our way."

"Mischief?" grunted the final man among them in their traveling group. "The evildoers are a bit more dangerous than such a word implies." Darnish gave a humorless smile. "At least we will have the element of surprise on our side if an attack occurs. Few men would assume someone as small as our daughter could fight better than many warriors."

"It would not matter if they suspected she was female; Creator spare us. She might be dressed the part, but she is certainly not acting like a trained warrior at the moment,"

Leodon asserted. "The girl lacks discipline and wisdom; I pity the grooms who win her hand."

Ellias sighed. "You speak the truth, but let us enjoy the thrill of watching her get into a few last bouts of trouble while we can. Soon she will be wed and move away. Life will be boring in the Village of Urijah then."

"I wager the village which gains her will offer to send her and it's warriors to live among our people once they realize what a disruptive, though beautiful, troublemaker we have raised." Darnish brushed a long, gray lock of hair off his square forehead before doubling his pace to catch up with their daughter.

All three men kept a watchful eye on the path around them, ready to respond to any threat that might arrive. The grounds outside the villages and around the city were lawless territory. Those banished from civilized settlements roamed these regions, preying on anyone passing by. To be captured by these evildoers meant certain death to any males and worse for any females.

Women were a rare, sought after commodity since war demolished most of humanity countless cycles before. Finding one outside the walls of the city or away from the protection of the village settlements was sporadic indeed. While male children were plentiful, treaties had to be brokered with the City of Women in order to win brides from within to help keep various lineages alive.

Stumbling upon a village born female was unheard of. Laws were strict about such matters. But Jemina often managed to find a way around any barriers attempting to limit her. When her twin brother Jael went off to train as a warrior, the imp managed to convince the elders of Urijah into allowing her to watch the preparation from afar. Separate from the boys training, she mimicked their every move. Then she practiced what she learned in the wee hours of the night until she could prove her worth to the council and seek approval to join the training.

Leodon grunted with frustration, recalling how he had put

his foot down when Jemina first sought permission to train alongside her twin. He argued a village born female was too valuable to risk possible injury during such vigorous training practices. But Jemina had been ready for such a hurdle. She was always prepared with a quick response to argue her point.

MANY CYCLES BEFORE

JEMINA PROUDLY STOOD before the elders, her radiant freckles dazzling her audience. Her windswept hair floated around her oval face as she spoke. Leodon could easily see there was no doubt lingering in her mind. She was convinced she would succeed in her latest, ridiculous quest. He saw the way Alistrair, the head Elder, was smiling down at her. Wise, he might be, but his wild hair and unkempt beard were better reflections of his true eccentric manner. The leader enjoyed Jemina's wild streak and was prone to humoring the girl.

"As a village daughter, I have more to fear than most." Her pale, steel blue eyes lowered a bit, as if in submission. When she lifted them again, they were full of fire. "Such is the reason I implore you to allow me a chance to learn the skills necessary to protect myself. The brave warriors who patrol our village boundaries are powerful and capable indeed, but breaches are not unheard of.

"Aye, I understand all too well the peril I face if evildoers manage to capture me. All I ask is an opportunity to learn the necessary means to protect myself until our brave warriors can come to my rescue." Her tone was silvery and demure. Her father had little doubt the elders found themselves ready to amend the rules for her, yet again.

Leodon stood up then, his triad at his sides. He remained

silent as Ellias spoke, but kept a wary eye on their daughter. He noticed Ellena, their wife, holding counsel with Jemina. It was an ominous sign. Though he loved the stunning woman he and his triad had claimed from the city, he was not blind to the sly manner in which she conducted herself, especially where their only daughter was concerned. Born in the city, Ellena felt restricted with life in the village.

Ellena was loyal to each of her three husbands and would never consider returning to the city; Leodon was sure of it. But their wife understood the thirst for adventure their only daughter had. Ellena had nurtured it from infancy. With a sly nod, he watched her signal for Jemina to keep her lips closed and not argue as her eldest father spoke to the council.

Leodon could almost hear his wife's warning. *"Blatantly challenging your fathers, especially in public, will not improve your chances to succeed."* Walking away, Jemina must have decided it was indeed wise to allow her mother to help her win favor with the council instead of arguing further.

Leodon watched as his wife signaled her desire to be recognized by the elders. Once given leave to speak, Ellena begged the council to allow her to conference in private with her husbands. "Pray, give me but a few moments to explain my thoughts on this matter to my mates. Before we explain our family unit's thinking on this matter, it is wise for us to come to a consensus. Don't you agree, Alistrair?"

Her husbands groaned, knowing they now faced a battle of wits more formidable than dealing with the village elders. But Alistrair had already called a recess of the meeting, leaving the family unit alone to battle it out.

Once she had them in private, Leodon watched as their beautiful wife began working to soothe the protective rage coursing through her mates' bodies. "My dear husbands, before you try to sway the council into rejecting our daughter's request, allow me a few moments to explain why I think supporting Jemina is a better decision.

Jael will protect his twin sister if any trouble should befall her during training sessions. Aside from his watchful eye, she will be safe because none of the other fledglings would do anything to chance hurting the only surviving village born daughter of Urijah for ten cycles. Our mischievous offspring has a wild side that puts her in danger inside the safety of our protective village. One day she will move away from us. I would feel more at ease knowing she could protect herself if trouble arises and her loving fathers are no longer available to save her."

"If?" Darnish quipped. "Ellena, surely you mean when? Trouble always follows our daughter. She thrives on it. Only the Creator could fathom why, but you encourage it."

"All the more reason to allow her to train." Ellena ran her hand under Darnish's silver beard, her fingers circling a patch of sensitive skin she assumed only she knew existed. His eyes widened and she did not have to reach down to check if his body had responded to her coaxing. Leodon scoffed at how easily his friend had been won over.

Jemina had inherited her mother's red hair, but while the younger female's was untamed, Ellena's was smooth and silky to the touch. Her mates had often said her beautiful hair had been one of the very things that made them select her when they had claimed their bride. One of the three was especially fond of her tresses. He liked to tug on them as he surged into her body. Leodon saw her brush the length against Ellias' bare shoulder as she turned her charm on him next.

As the oldest and leader of the family, it was Ellias' duty to be the voice of reason. Leodon silently bid his fellow husband to stay strong. It was a wasted plea. Once their wife pushed her hair back and exposed her neck, the leader of their family unit could not take his eyes off the delicate, pale skin. "Aye, Jemina's twin and the other fledglings will protect her with their lives. We cannot watch over her day and night. As a fledgling, she would be too busy training to run us haggard."

Leodon threw up his hands, determined to stay impassive until the matter was resolved and Jemina's welfare guaranteed. He crossed his thick arms across his massive chest and mocked his triad with a raised, bushy eyebrow. They had no inkling they had been manipulated. He swore to himself that he would remain focused on their daughter's fate and not his hard cock.

As if she could read his expression, Ellena addressed his fears. "What if someone did manage to breach the protection of our village? Wouldn't you feel better knowing our daughter could protect me and our younger children when you rushed off to fight our enemies?"

Ellena turned to face the others after gauging his reaction. She accidently backed into him, and Leodon groaned loudly. The soft globes of her backside rubbed against his hard thighs. Stiffening his stance, he vowed to stay his set course. Her long hair swept across his bare chest as she turned her head to apologize for backing into him. But damn if she didn't lift her backside higher until it rubbed against his swollen erection. She flexed the muscles in her ass and his manhood swelled eagerly.

Though middle aged, his lovely wife could arouse him with a mere glance. Getting her back to their home and undressed soon pushed any thought about protesting Jemina's training away. Ellias was right. With Jemina training as a fledgling, the husbands and wife could catch up on more intimate pursuits. Besides, what harm could come of letting her train. Village born females where confined to the boundaries of the village of Urijah. Not until potential mates came here, to compete for the gift of claiming her as their village bride, would she be in any real danger.

"Ellias, as leader, it is your responsibility to share our family unit's desires, I mean thinking on the matter of Jemina training. Take your time explaining. Darnish and I will be with our dear wife in her center room. Join us when you can."

JEMINA'S blue eyes darted about, trying to drink in everything around her. The whole lot was so green and free. Branches sprouted off of trees, no meaningful order to their direction. The sounds of wild creatures in the distance had her wondering what kind of animals she might finally get to see. Oh, the warriors who hunted for the village often brought in various beasts, but they were limp and cold when she finally got to examine them. What would it be like to touch a warm, wild, living creature?

Wild cats roamed this area, if her brother Jael was to be believed. They flashed sharp teeth and thrived on ripping flesh from the body of anyone crazy enough to stumble within reach. Jemina did not bother to fret on the matter. Jael also thought the healer Dalia's dogs were dangerous beings. So did many of the other fledglings and even a fair number of warriors back in their village.

It was pure nonsense, she knew. With a little meat and patience, Jemina had managed to win over the healer's alpha male hound. The others followed his lead, accepting her and allowing her to pet them and lead them around. Why the image of the Elder Alistrair suddenly popped in her head, she knew not. Probably because the dominant dog was furious looking too, but once won over, a loveable creature at heart.

Giggling, she remembered the time she had led a large pack of the dogs into the barracks where the fledglings lived. She had tried to convince the elders into allowing her to live among the others who trained beside her. Until that moment, she had assumed the others were her friends and allies, but they proved they were traitorous beasts at the meeting. As a united group, with Jael of all people as their spokesperson, the men she trained alongside demanded Jemina be banned from even entering the area where they rested at night.

The elders had sided with the boys, no doubt, Jemina realized, because she had forgotten to act demure and obedient while in their presence. In her disgust with the other fledglings' betrayal, she had started chasing after various young men, threatening to use her sword to unman them for their mean words. The elders had laughed at the sight of a wee girl raging at young men who were supposed to be future warriors.

It had been Alistrair, the leader of the elders, who raised his hand to end the chase. "There are some places daughters cannot go, sweet Jemina. It is time you learn this hard fact." Though he had weather-beaten skin and a penetrating voice, she did not flinch at his words. Rarely did Alistrair deny her wishes, and it hurt her pride to have him side with the others now.

"Just as there are places where men are not accepted?" she asked boldly, when Jael started to sanction her, Alistrair raised a hand to halt him. "How often have you warned the villagers about the wrongness of the city dwellers who separate themselves from others merely by gender, sir? If their action is wrong, wouldn't stopping me from living with the fledglings be just as wrong?"

She had not been trying to shame him, as some of the other elders were quick to assume. She truly sought to understand the leader's reasoning, for she valued his opinion above all others, save for her mother. Alistrair knew this and walked over to stand before her. "No men are allowed inside the city's inner wall. Ever. This is not true of women entering the fledglings' barracks."

"So I may move there?" She knew his answer before he spoke. His warm, wide set eyes were easy to read. "If women are allowed to enter, why not me?"

"Unlike you, the women who go to the fledglings' beds are there to do an important task. They help train our future warriors for a job you will never have to concern yourself about. Has your mother or fathers not yet explained the purpose of the cast-offs who service our village?"

Jemina was confused by his words. She reflected on what little she did know about the cast-offs. There was a group of women who lived off on their own, without a triad of fathers to boss them around. The men in the village often smiled at these ladies, though never if a wife was around to witness such affection to someone not of their family unit. Alistrair seemed to ponder if he should provide more information or send her back to her parents for them to do so.

"Please explain their duty, sir. I am not a small child anymore. In a few years, warriors will come here hoping to claim me as a bride. I do not wish to be ignorant of important matters involving our customs."

Her words touched him. "They show the fledglings how to please a bride, Jemina. Your future husbands are no doubt being trained by their village's version of this system. It is a very private and complex ritual, one that an innocent, village daughter, soon to be a village bride, need not witness."

It was futile to continue arguing, but Jemina often dared to question matters on the off-chance things might change. "Don't I need to learn how to please my future mates? Maybe I can watch from afar, as I did when I first observed the training sessions for battle?" A collected gasp of outrage filled the meeting area, both from her fellow fledglings and the council elders.

Alistrair turned to stare the others into silence. Then he grasped Jemina's hand and offered some words of wisdom she would remember forever. "It is not your job to please your husbands, my sweet Jemina. As their bride, your mates are responsible for making you happy, not the other way around. It is one of the few powers a woman holds in the villages. The other women will not thank you for challenging it. This matter is closed. You don't have to like the outcome, but I expect you to respect it and drop all talk on moving into the fledgling's barracks."

Jemina had conceded then, not wanting to turn the women against her, nor chance having Alistrair harden his heart on any future pleas she might make. But she was determined to prove herself equal to the others who trained alongside her. She was just as brave and skilled as they were. Their small victory might make them think she was weaker, she reasoned. Jemina used bits of meat to lead the healer's most threatening looking hounds toward their barracks where the fledglings slept. Then she coaxed them inside, being careful not to cross the threshold herself. Aye, she respected Alistrair's decision, even if she did not like it one bit.

She sat back on the green grass surrounding the fields where they trained for battle. She waited patiently, sure Jael and the others would notice their new visitors soon enough. They would have to admit she was braver than they when it came to dealing with the hounds.

Within minutes, loud shouts of alarm filled the air. But it wasn't her fellow fledglings running from the building, but several cast-off women. Jemina's small mouth popped open as she realized they were in various stages of undress. The dogs, thinking the runners were playing a game with them, gave chase.

Soon her fellow fledglings emerged, many with exposed portions of their bodies that Jemina had never seen before. While she had helped to care for her baby brothers, it had not prepared her for the sight of a grown-up version of what hung below the pants men wore.

Jemina had planned to run toward the fray, sword raised to drive off the dogs with her friends, but it was out of the question now. Closing her eyes, she prayed none of the dogs got hurt because of her poorly planned plot. She was sure she never wanted to see another grown man naked again.

THREE YEARS HAD PASSED since that time. Jemina had not hit puberty when it had transpired, but within a few months, she discovered her interest in the opposite sex was healthy, though sorely challenged. It was impossible to look upon the boys she grew up with as anything but brothers. The full-grown warriors were all matched up with city brides. Besides, people within the village were related through the common ancestor of Urijah. She was not meant to mate with any of them. She dreamed of mysterious men, from far off settlements, who were trained to please a woman. In her dreams, she had strong opinions about what they would look like and how they would act. One must have sky blue eyes. Auburn-hair, pulled tight with a leather strap at the base of a thick neck. The leader would be a gentle lover, one who learned about making love alongside her instead of finding his way with a slew of cast-off women.

Soon she would have men competing for the honor of claiming her as a bride. Jemina was eager to wield the power her mother and the other village wives already held. She would have three husbands whose duty it was to please her. Parts of her body tingled eagerly at the mere idea. If her fathers were not mere feet away, she would dare to stroke herself as she fantasized of the pleasure awaiting her.

2

Aras: Bound but Resolved

Jasper and Barden eagerly started to gather their various weapons that hung on the exterior wall of the city. Then they started collecting what sparse belongings each had in preparation for the approaching opening that led to the next wall surrounding the city. Aras put off the task, dreading moving another cycle closer to their doomed fate. Had they already completed two cycles of their three rotations? Their duty was clear. Their triad helped to shield the city of females, which had long ago insisted on separating itself from the three outer villages.

History suggested the female leaders within blamed the men for causing the war, which had nearly caused the extinction of humans many cycles before. At first, the few survivors, men and women, had bonded together after the disaster. Slowly they started rebuilding, forming small communities. A strict code of behavior was established, and those who did not follow the rules were exiled.

The communities flourished, but when men started developing weapons and showing signs of aggression, most of the women had quickly departed to establish their own community.

Within their peaceful community, fighting was outlawed. Citizens worked for the common good. Weapons and males were forbidden. The women even built a tall wall around their city to keep the hostiles, as they labeled all men, out.

The male village elders had ordered two more walls built around the city of fools. They understood the threat of those evildoers from outside the villages was real; even if the city women did not admit as much, nor have sense enough to prepare a proper defense. The women inside were guilty of clinging to the naïve belief that their puny wall would protect those within it.

Eventually, the elders of the various villages reasoned, the women would finally realize how precarious their situation was and agree to soften their stance on the topic of protection. Even talented healers from the city had abandoned it, preferring to settle close to the village people who needed their skills.

It took numerous cycles before the prediction had come to pass, but eventually the city had been forced to acknowledge the flaw in their oversight regarding defense. The leaders of the women, called priestess of all labels, finally lowered themselves to broker a deal with those they labeled as hostiles. If the village men agreed to protect the three walls surrounding their city, provide small provisions of meat to supplement the mostly vegetarian diet of those inside the walls, and share fuel rations to help power their factories, the city would allow the villages to select a limited number of brides from a group of young ladies offered at the end of each cycle.

The proposition had come at a time when the village leaders realized their already small number of female citizens was dwindling fast. While those inside the city seemed to have mastered a process of reproducing without need of traditional means, the villages still depended on the old-fashioned coupling method.

Barden sighed. His boyish face had only a few whiskers despite being many cycles since he had shaved. Others often mocked him for this youth, so he often tried to dispel the notion with crude talk. "One more cycle of service, and we shall finally be considered warriors. I cannot wait for the honor."

Taking a seat on a rock near the two other men with him, he continued, "I find myself trying to picture the young woman we will select. Will she have a fair or dark complexion? I hope her locks are long, as well as her legs. In truth, I am desperate with need for the chance to bed our chosen bride. It has been too many cycles without the glory of sheathing myself in the warmth of a wet, hot core."

Directly to his right, Jasper reached over and cuffed Barden across the back of his dark head. "Speak with respect when talking about our future bride. She won't be some cast-off, showing dozens of fledglings the ways of pleasing a woman. Our bride will be untouched and pure, deserving of respect and protection."

Jasper's boyish features were hidden behind a full mustache and beard. As the oldest, it was his duty to lead his triad and help them grow into the type of warriors which would not only represent the Village of Konrad with honor, but also be the bridegrooms any woman would hope for. "You should try to adapt our friend Aras' mature demeanor. He honors his duty quietly and awaits the glory of coupling with our bride without a word."

Barden chuckled as he rubbed the sting out of the back of his head. "Aras doesn't speak of bedding any women, cast-off or not. Some claim our fellow triad member is as pure as those inside the city. Why is that, I wonder?"

Boldly studying his friend's face, Barden seemed to be waiting to see if Aras would attack him or finally explain why he was so void of emotion about the thrill of protecting the city and claiming their mate. Even Jasper gave the impression he was holding his breath, hoping for some insight. But the last member of their triad remained quiet.

Aras did not even acknowledge the question. He never spoke

of his personal feelings, learning long ago to hold them in for fear that he might unknowingly mention something he shouldn't. The family unit he came from had adopted the standoffish manner cycles before, after tragedy struck them and tore their family apart. One day, together with his fathers, the injustice done to them would be addressed. But it was not the time or place to discuss the matter now.

Until that time, he held himself apart from others, even the members of his own triad. Jasper and Barden were his friends. He would protect them at the expense of his own life, if necessary. Aside from his own brother Loinbard, these two men were his closest friends. Yet they had different goals in life, and a blissful ignorance of the evil truth behind earning the right to claim a city bride. He felt like a traitor for not warning them of the danger ahead and the pain their current path promised, yet doing so might jeopardize the careful plan his fathers had laid out cycles ago to avenge their family unit's tragedy.

One day soon, Aras promised himself, he would tell all who would listen about the horrible betrayal the city of women was playing on the naïve villagers who protected their walls. One day, there would be hell to pay. He would find a way to survive whatever challenges lay ahead of him, until then he'd remain quiet.

An unexpected sound from the outer wall brought all three men to attention. Each grabbed a sharp sword and positioned themselves to prevent any breach. The secret section, which opened from this circle to the next, was not due to be unlocked for two more new sunrises. Aras pondered if the outer wall might have been penetrated by evildoers seeking to take over the city. Had he not been honor bound to protect the wall, he might savor watching them bring down the city leaders. Innocent lives were at stake, though. As far as he knew, only the women addressed as priestess were responsible for the travesty that brought death in its wake.

"Descendants of Konrad, lower your weapons. Our elder has

arrived and wishes to meet with all before the changing of walls tomorrow." Recognizing the voice of a fellow warrior called Roan, Aras and the others cautiously relaxed their attack stance, but each kept their guard up waiting for confirmation there was no threat present.

The weathered, but friendly face of their Chief Elder Otto came into view as the surreptitious entrance parted. "Greetings, friends. It has been a long time since we last spoke. I hope all is well with your triad."

Jaspar returned his weapon to its sheath at his side and rushed forward to shake the wrinkled hand of the leader. Barden's comical grin secretly mocked the reverence their friend showed, but he soon followed suit. Aras was the last to move forward, first studying those at the entrance carefully.

Tradition was paramount in the Village of Konrad. Though they were stationed miles away from home, outside the city, this territory was deemed an extension of Konrad land. Changes to schedules and events meant something unusual was afoot. Had the secret his family had been guarding all these cycles finally come to light? News from home was sparse at the wall. During the three cycle absences, many things could transpire without the men at the wall knowing about them.

The gray-headed leader stepped away from the gate entrance. "Ah, my dear Aras, you are still the solemn soul I left here two years ago. I had hoped time away from your family and friends would mellow your serious demeanor."

Honor bound to show respect; Aras gave a slight bend at the waist before putting away his sword to shake hands with the elder. "What news from my family and friends do you bring, sir? All are well, I assume."

"Your family unit has grown yet again," Otto said. "Attie brought forth another son. As with the other three babes she blessed the Village of Konrad with, she opted to deliver at home.

Strange, that choice, don't you think? Might you have any insight into this decision?"

Aras' family unit was the first in generations to refuse using the healer's hut when the time came to bring forth a new life. The village elders voiced concern often, expressing fear other mothers might follow suit. Many young mothers suffered significant blood loss during childbirth. Though rare, death resulted if the bleeding could not be controlled properly. The rulers felt having the healer deliver babies was the best practice.

Aras said bluntly, "Babies have been known to disappear from the healer's delivery room. After losing her first-born child there, I imagine my second mother is more comfortable being home with my fathers at her side, ensuring her and their babies' protection."

"Your fathers are not trained in the ways of a healer," the older man pointed out.

"Yet they have managed to deliver her babies without consequence. I am sure Ulthia hovered close by in case there was a need for her services." Aras tried to keep the disgust in his voice to a minimum as he spoke the name.

At one time, the Konrad healer had stepped in to raise him and his younger brothers after his birth mother died and his only surviving birth father, Ryder had been ordered to protect the city wall. Yet he could not overlook the insult the healer helped perpetrate on his family and the village of Konrad.

"What brings you here, two days ahead of schedule, sir? Surely you did not come all this way to announce the birth of another village son. A village daughter, maybe, but a son, unlikely…" he said.

"Every birth is an event to rejoice and celebrate, Aras, though it would be wonderful to welcome a village daughter after all these cycles of drought." Otto gestured for Barden and Jasper to join them. "I bring special visitors. Members from the Village of Urijah have come to make an important announcement. They wait outside the last wall. Without the blessings of Omo, I cannot open the inner most gate to invite the first-year fledglings to join us, but you three will not want to miss this important news."

Leaving behind their belongings, the triad followed the elder through the gate, down a long path and through another opening in another wall. Seated by a small fire, several groups of people sat, chatting gaily. Aras' lips thinned. As if knowing his own village was cursed was not troubling enough, seeing the strange colors of another village made his stomach knot. As far as he was aware, there were at least three established villages that guarded the city of women. Each was likely affected by the same, hideous secret, yet all were clueless of what was happening.

He watched the others laugh, heard the whispers of claiming brides and the honor of starting a family unit. It disgusted him. His friends, men he had trained alongside of for cycles, spoke in awe of earning the right to claim a bride. How he wanted to shout about the injustice of the entire process, and the heartache they would soon discover.

Aras' eyes came to rest on the smallest of the foreigners visiting their camp. Though facing away from him, it was obvious from the slight figure that this fledgling was more child than warrior. It was unfair to force the reality of adulthood on someone so young. The boy should be home, playing with his friends, instead of speaking about claiming a city bride.

"Is the Village of Urijah hurting for sons? Please tell me you are not seriously considering sending babes to service along the walls your village is responsible for protecting."

He had not meant to say the words aloud, but the eerie silence that followed told Aras his insult had not gone unnoticed. Three of the four strangers stood up and turned his way, their hands immediately going to rest on the weapons at their sides. Otto muttered a soft curse and came to stand behind Aras in a show of grudging support.

"Excuse my rude words." Aras swallowed his pride and

reminded himself of his duty. "I fear the isolation of life on the wall has dulled my wisdom. Please accept my apology." He walked toward the fire, his triad and elder only one step behind, to offer his hand to the fledgling he had just disrespected, hoping the older men beside the stranger did not attack before he made amends.

The slender figure slowly stood and turned to meet his eyes. Aras' step faltered and his mouth dropped opened. "You're a woman!" he noted in awe. "But women aren't allowed outside the safety of village borders."

"It would seem your cycles of isolation at the city walls has indeed dulled your thinking, sir." Radiant freckles and glorious windswept hair the color of fire greeted him as a pixie-faced beauty raged at him.

"First, you assume our village would send children to protect the city walls, and now you appear to not trust your own eyes about matters of gender. Tis the truth: I am indeed a woman, a village born one at that. While your village may not prepare its citizens in the ways of protecting themselves, the elders of Urijah do, as evidence of my presence here, outside of our border."

Once her speech was given, the spitfire brought her hands up to rest on her slender hips, and Aras felt his heart seize for a moment. He thought she was about to lay into him yet again with her sharp tongue, when she suddenly blinked her eyes at him in alarm.

She stared at him for a moment before searching behind him. Thinking his triad or the elder might have shown some sign of aggression, Aras turned to warn them off. But he found them smiling at his being taken to task by a mere woman, not trying to support him in any manner. Turning back, he wondered at her sudden loss of words.

He reflected on the things she had said. One statement kept echoing in his ear. *"I am indeed a woman, a village born one at that."*

Irony had struck again. There was but one way a triad could

avoid the heartache of claiming a bride without chancing the deadly curse. A village bride did not carry the same plague some of the city brides did. But village born brides were almost impossible to find, and an unattached triad discovering an available one when she was of age to marry was rare. Yet here she was, the most beautiful woman he had ever set eyes on, old enough to have grooms fight for her hand in marriage. And he had just insulted her, and by the looks of the angry men beside her, her fathers, too.

3

Loinbard: Defiantly Free

"She is still moping over the rude Konrad's insult," Leodon said. "We should have killed the boy before leaving the Konrad section of wall."

"And chance starting a war with one of our closest allies?" Darnish countered.

"I am sure the dozen or so other Konrads sitting nearby might have thought to intervene had we attacked," Ellias pointed out.

"Then we should have left him with a small reminder to think before he speaks next time. A wee little scar from cheek to cheek," Leodon chuckled. "What say you, daughter?"

Jemina forged a smile. Giving him a tight hug, she showed her appreciation for his concern. "Do not fret, Papa. I believe his slight did not go unchecked. Mother taught me early on about ways to inflict pain without pulling out a sharp sword. Sometimes a curt word, delivered before the offender's closest comrades, imposes a deeper wound, which is slower to scab over."

The path they followed through the dense forest was plush with beautiful trees, vines and flowers. The three men laughed and eventually started discussing other matters, and Jemina was grateful. It left her free to dwell on her own thoughts. For cycles now, she had dreamed of three men who would fight for the right to claim her as their bride. The faces of two of her mates were so clear in her visions, Jemina almost remembered their every feature. She had thought it was her unconscious mind creating a composite for the type of men whom she would be attracted to one day.

Then the first man of her vivid dreams materialized before her eyes at the Konrad wall. He was always her first husband in the visions. Solemn, but patient with her as they learned the glory of making love. Suddenly he had sprung to life and stood mere feet away from her by the fire. Hooded sapphire eyes, once dark hair now bleached from the sun draping over his strong forehead, the man the elder Otto called Aras, might very well have walked out of one of her vivid dreams.

Her eyes had sought the remaining members of his triad for confirmation. She thought to find a handsome man with caramel hair and piercing sky-blue eyes and a fetching man with thick, blond hair tamed only by a strong, leather strap holding much of it at the base of his broad neck. Instead she saw two attractive, but boyish looking men. They were definitely not the men she associated with Aras.

All these cycles she had put stock in finding the perfect men of her dreams. Now the Creator seemed to be mocking her, proving finding the mates of her heart was futile, something only a child would hope to achieve. Aras, how she loved that name, was a member of a triad that bore no similarity to the one she had envisioned. Even his arrogant manner was contrary to the devoted, tender lover she had created in her sleeping mind. Her presence outside of the safety of a village clearly irritated him. He was not likely to leave a sure thing like the promise of city bride to come compete for the mere chance of winning a village one.

Maybe the three men of her dreams were not meant to be

considered as a triad after all. Each could represent her desires in a mate. If Aras was not her fated mate, maybe she should look for one of the other two men of her visions. The next stop on their journey was to be the Konrad village itself. Hopefully she would receive a more welcoming greeting from the people there than Aras had offered. If not, she would do well to put her hopes in the Village of Finn. They were known for their blond locks and handsome faces. Surely the blond member of her dream triad would come from that region. Not wanting to jinx her luck as she had with Aras, Jemina promised herself she would be very pleasant to anyone who might fit the description of one of her dream mates.

At the gathering area of the Konrad village, she found another dream mate. From the side, he favored Aras in many ways. They bore the same strong jaw and thin, pale lips. The moment one of the chieftains declared Jemina was a village born bride seeking potential mates to compete for her hand in marriage, the tall stranger pushed his way through the tight knot of people blocking his path. He did not stop until he was directly in front of her as she stood on a platform. Then a winning smile lit his face and her heart started pounding excitedly. He was the third husband in her fantasies.

Before her fathers could protest, the man reached for her hand and pressed a kiss to its palm. A blush crept across her face as she felt his tongue dart out to taste her skin. "Your beauty is rarer than your position as a village born bride. I fear anyone hoping to win your hand will have to fight off countless suitors."

Leodon stepped between the couple then and used his heavy frame to block the young man's access to her. "You would be wise to fear three overprotective fathers before concerning yourself with any other suitors, young man."

"With a daughter as breathtaking as yours, sir, I respect your protective nature. I am called Loinbard, from the family unit of Ryder, Wolf, Kia and Attie."

Ellias stepped down from the small platform in the center of the meeting area. Darnish did likewise and started interrogating the young man. "You speak of a family unit instead of boasting of your triad. Are we to assume you lost your fellow mates at such a youthful age?"

Jemina rose on her toes, trying to get a better look at this Loinbard. His eyes were indeed sky-blue and the pupils were large as he dared to lock eyes with her despite being surrounded by her hostile fathers. On impulse, she lifted her tiny hand and gave a friendly wave, returning his welcoming smile.

Ellias grew frustrated at the continued flirting and used his wide shoulder to nudge the younger man's attention back to her fathers. "Tis the truth that it is unusual for a village bride to be present when her fathers announce her availability for marriage, but the rules of such proclamations still stand. You will direct any interest you might have in competing for her hand to us. We will then decide if you warrant an invitation to contend for our daughter's hand. Where is your triad, son?"

"I have no triad, sir," Loinbard announced without shame, and Jemina could not help but feel let down again. Her fathers were sure to reject a single suitor outright, fearing she would be left alone if a sole mate was slain.

"You are of age," Darnish continued. "Why aren't you at the wall now? Are the fledglings in this village so plentiful that able-bodied sons don't have to do their duty for the purpose of selecting a bride?"

The elder who had been overseeing the announcement intervened between them, but not before giving Loinbard a stern glare. "He is the second born son of his family unit. His older brother spent many years trying to form a triad with Loinbard without success. They trained together, and truth be known, both are among the finest warriors our village has ever boasted. But Loinbard refuses to service three years of commitment at the city in order to gain a wife. Instead, he has always sworn to wait until a suitable village born bride becomes available."

As the elder's proclamation slowly filtered through her brain, Jemina found herself becoming outraged. Climbing down from the platform was not as easy for her, as she was barely five-foot-tall, but she refused the helping hand of those around her. Slipping between the frames of her imposing fathers, she came to stand toe to toe with Loinbard.

"How dare you try to convince me you were captivated by my 'rare' beauty. You've been waiting for a village bride to become available, and she could be a hideous creature as far as you were concerned."

He dared to chuckle at her outrage. "Your inner fire pleases me, lovely Jemina. Too many women from my village are afraid to stand up for themselves. Know that if I have the honor of winning your hand, I respect strong women. My mother, Attie is much the same way as you are. She keeps my fathers on their toes. There are foolish men who prefer meek wives. I am not one of them."

Was she doomed to see the third dream lover from her fantasies eliminated from the competition already? First Aras proved unsuitable, now Loinbard's lack of a triad eradicated his chances. Maybe the Creator was punishing her for coming along on this mission? Then again, there were countless sins from her past the heavens might be paying her back for now. "Without a triad, you have little chance of winning my hand," she said, pretending not to be thrilled by his earlier words of praise.

"If being part of a triad is required, sweet Jemina, I must set out at haste to align myself with one immediately." Loinbard reached up to run his finger down her cheek before Darnish shoved him aside.

JEMINA SAW HIS HAIR FIRST. It was a glorious mass of golden silk. Her fathers beckoned her to the center of the Village of Finn's gathering area, but she was reluctant to move on. The first two men of her dream lovers had been snatched away from her so soon. First Aras, the bleached blond gentle lover turned judgmental brute. Then Loinbard, the caramel-headed, sky blue-eyed seducer had been revealed as only a desperate man searching a rare prize. How would this dream mate stray from perfection?

Women, young and old, jostled about in an effort to get close to where the man she sought stood. Cast-offs, Jemina decided. No village born woman would be allowed to show such public affection. Certainly, no mated wife would get away with such open admiration of another male, she reasoned.

Two other men, likely the admired man's triad sat quietly a row in front of him. They carried satchels and a few weapons with them. Nodding to herself, Jemina concluded the three were off to begin their first year of serving on the walls of the city. A ray of hope shined in her heart. Going to the city meant the golden hair man was old enough and brave enough to challenge for her hand in marriage. Before allowing herself to get overly excited, Jemina decided to get a better look at the man's features.

Waiting anxiously, she positioned herself carefully and waited for the women surrounding him to part so she might have a better look. In her dreams, his face was always cast in shadows as he moved his tongue along her body, suckling, nipping and kissing various sensitive areas. Just recalling the sensations had her growing damp. *Please, oh great Creator, don't let me be disappointed yet again.*

At the center of the gathering area, a man, no doubt the more powerful of the village elders, spoke. Finally, the women reluctantly moved aside to take their seats, and Jemina got her first peek at the man she observed. She gasped. He was indeed glorious. In old earth time, surely this would be one of the beautiful people whose only task was to pose for great artists. His chiseled features were perfection. She would do her best not to disqualify this candidate.

When the time came to depart for the portion of the wall where the Village of Finn's men guarded the city, Jemina convinced her fathers to travel with the elder and triad ready to begin their service on the wall. No women were allowed away from the safety of the community boundaries, and she finally had time alone with the handsome man named Crosby.

He did not converse much, spending most of the time smiling down at her. At first his silence irked Jemina but then she recalled speaking had led to the first two dream mates eliminating themselves as possible husbands. Grabbing Crosby's large hand in her own, she allowed herself to enjoy his beauty. She chatted away happily, telling him about her village and her skills with a sword.

While distracted with this potential husband, she did not notice the others in their party were on full alert. Two vanished, one to the west and one to the east, as they traveled along. A terrifying growl split the air, and Jemina searched for its source, freeing her weapon. A tawny, lean creature, bigger than any hound the Healer of Urijah owned, was perched on a boulder a few yards ahead of them. For a moment, she wished she had brought her own pet on this journey. Smiley would chase off any threats. Then the magnificent animal before her flexed the muscles along its broad shoulders, and she longed to get a closer look. The yellow teeth on display when it roared again gave her pause. Could this creature be tamed? Might she be able to lure it back to her village and spend time observing its behavior and winning its trust? Dalia, the healer from her village claimed Jemina had a talent with all manner of beasts. Then again, she tried to convince the village daughter that she had some special gift called The Sight. The only glimpse into the future Jemina had ever seen involved her three husbands. Apparently, her gift of sight needed adjustments.

The creature prepared to pounce as she walked closer. Her

fathers yanked her behind them, and she protested loudly. Time seemed to slow down suddenly. She watched in horror as the creature leapt into the air, sharp claws ready to tear flesh from bone. Her fathers would surely be killed. But before the animal could land, two figures rushed from the sides and launched themselves up to pierce the animal's neck and belly. It screamed in anger and pain.

Pushing past her fathers, she rushed to where the creature now lay, the other members of Crosby's triad at its sides, still on high alert in case the animal tried to attack again. Jemina's eyes sought Crosby's briefly. He seemed as startled by the course of events as she had been. Returning her attention to the animal, she noted it was probably one of the feline creatures her brother Jael had spoken of. Fresh blood stained its coat as it's life slowly slipped away.

4

Anders: Freed Without a Voice

The journey to the wall where the Finn warriors guarded was far enough to require one night of rest outside in the forbidden territories between villages and city. Jemina rested in a small tent erected by her fathers, wrapped in soft blankets they had brought along for her comfort. Outside the tent, her fathers formed a protective triangle, using their supine bodies to block anyone from getting inside. Next to them, Enoch, the village elder from Finn and the triad traveling with him formed another defending barrier. Safe from worry, Jemina fell into a deep sleep. Her dream lovers visited her again, mocking her with visions of a life she would never gain.

"SPREAD YOUR LEGS WIDER, wife. We wish to view your treasures." The command came from Aras. He had a hint of a smile touching his lips. Jemina longed to find a way to make him let down his guard.

"It is unfair for you three to gawk at my naked form while you stand their fully clad," she protested. Being married was still new to her. True, she

understood much of the details associated with making love now, but she was still shy about being naked in front of three men.

"Our bride wants us to undress," Loinbard teased, slowly pulling off his clothing. The auburn-haired husband and Aras followed his lead. Soon, three very aroused men were standing before her, waiting for her to spread her legs. A mixture of emotions washed through her body. Her pale skin was flushed with embarrassment. Her heart was beating quickly, yet her breathing was slow and steady. How could something so immodest feel right?

Slowly her slender legs fell open, and she thrilled when the three men moved a bit closer so they could gain a better view. Their words added to her heightened awareness of how sensitive every nerve ending on her body felt at this very moment.

"So small and delicate," Aras noted. "How does she manage to accommodate each of us, yet remain so tight?"

"I haven't even gotten to the part of her which welcomes our seed," Loinbard muttered. "My eyes can't get past the tight patch of curls just above. It's the same shade of red as the beautiful hair framing her face. I long to inhale her sweet scent."

Her second husband's auburn mane hung over his face as he stepped forward, boldly reaching to pull her closer to the edge of bed. He positioned her knees until they helped lay her most private region wide and ready for access. "Soon you will relish more than her wonderful smell. If you follow my instructions properly, you will hear her soft moans of pleasure, see her fingers tear at the sheets, feel her clit swell, and taste her response to your efforts."

Hunching on his knees, he found a position that suited his requirements. His upper body leaned forward, yet he was still not pleased with his ability to reach her body. Strong arms reached under her shaky legs and yanked her closer to the foot of the bed. This warrior offered a deep groan signaling his contentment when he was finished.

Jemina flinched with surprise as his thick fingers started moving around her skin. He carefully explained various facts to his fellow husbands. He exposed what lay shielded within the sensitive folds below. His finger dipped ever so slightly into her wet channel. "While we may think this is the area to concentrate our efforts since it is what we associate with making love, the true heart of her enjoyment is just here."

He pulled back the hood of her clit and the cool air made Jemina clutch the sheets tightly. "The bud itself is extremely sensitive, so use a gentle, light touch to begin with." Each of her husbands took turns locating the delicate area, first removing its delicate covering, then barely exploring the nub.

Aras, ever the conscious learner, asked for more information. "Do we use our finger or tongue to initiate the first contact?"

"Both," the teacher explained, "but this section is our final goal, not where we will start our efforts to please her. In my experience, women prefer the subtle buildup of a thorough lover. We want our beautiful wife to have time to enjoy the sensations our efforts create. Don't rush the experience, and you will be rewarded with a more intense reaction from her by the end."

He carefully detailed a step by step guide, first telling, then showing with his actions. "Her inner thighs are a good place to start. Use your fingers to run across the smooth skin. Explore one side completely before moving to the next. Watch her face and make note of any indication of areas that invoke the strongest response. We want to learn her pleasure triggers."

Jemina enjoyed discovering secrets about her own body and the instruction continued. "Our tongues provide a different sensation. The texture is different and even the temperature. Use the knowledge of what you learned from stroking with your hand to focus your attention when you explore with your mouth."

"Must we always apply a gentle touch?" Loinbard bent down to watch Anders gentle teasing. "I have noticed our sweet Jem moans after a playful nip on her neck or even an aggressive tug at her pert little nipples."

Jemina watched her auburn-haired lover move aside, indicating for the younger husband to take his place. "Let's find out. Show us your technique. Aras and I will keep a close eye on our wife's reaction. Between the three of us, we will understand how her body responds better than even she does."

She did indeed enjoy a hint of rough play, tensing and moaning when it was delivered at moments she least expected it. Each worked on the skill of using their hands and mouths to please her. It had been Aras who had brought her to completion as the auburn-haired husband urged him to suckle, then dart his hot tongue across her clit. Basking in the glow of her desire, she found herself lifted back on the bed carefully. Each husband waited his turn to lie between her legs and spill seed deep inside her womb.

Morning arrived too quickly. Jemina longed to enjoy a few moments more of her sweet dream. Why would the Creator tease her with visions of Aras and Loinbard, two men no longer available to her as husband? It did not surprise her that Crosby's face was lacking from the dream. After spending time with the Finn warrior, Jemina was sure he was not the third man of her dreams. He lacked the experience and power she associated with the person.

WORD REACHED the fledglings of Finn before Jemina's party reached the wall. A village bride was seeking triads to compete for the honor of winning her as a wife. Those along the wall were clustered by triads, discussing the situation.

Anders tried to reason with the others in his group, but as usual, they were set on doing things their own way. "You are willing to walk away after three years of service, with the promise of a bride only hours away, for the mere chance of winning the hand of a village bride?"

Hendrix, who considered himself leader of their triad despite Anders' rightful position as such, spoke with disdain. "Why would we settle for a mere city bride when a rare, more valued village bride is available? As for having to compete for her, are we not the best warriors from the whole region?"

Exhaling deeply, Anders tried to maintain his already frayed patience. "We have yet to see the entire region. As skilled as we are, we have yet to be put to the test." The ginger-headed leader of the triad could not help but to again question why he had allowed himself to be pressured into forming a union with Hendrix and Johan. As fledglings, the two brothers had proved themselves to be talented with all manner of weapons, but they were self-serving and lacked real discipline. No third fledgling would agree to bond with them.

The village elders approached Anders, begging him to take on the leading position of the pair. In truth, none of the other groups of men trying to form triads felt like a proper fit for Anders so he allowed himself to be talked into taking on the two loners. He assumed, with time and maturity, the two would learn to look beyond superficial gains and work toward more long-term goals. He was wrong.

"Soon the city wall will open and three ladies will appear. From them, we can select which is best suited for life as our wife. I, myself, seek to find a woman who might be an asset to our village, one who would want the adventure of living outside of the city walls and want to start a life with us, raising strong, happy children," Anders reasoned.

Johan broke his silence. "The thrill of having our pick of mates is not lost on us. Hendrix and I already discussed what kind of wife we would select. I want the one with the biggest breasts. He wants a full backside. Both qualities matter not, now. No matter what she looks like, a village born bride is worth the sacrifice. We can always seek pleasure from the cast-offs if our new bride does not satisfy our needs."

The mere suggestion appalled Anders. To seek pleasure from a cast-off after a wedding was unfair to all involved. It was an insult to a wife, would bring shame to a family unit and was a misuse of the women tasked with instructing the men on ways to please a wife. He would never break a commitment for personal gain or self-pleasure.

Hendrix nodded showing his approval with his blood brother's logic. "Even if she is head strong, between the three of us, we can control one woman. It is worth the sacrifice. Our children will know exactly where their lineage comes from. The house of Finn will boast pure blood descendants from our family unit.

That fact alone will make all the difference when it is time for a new group of elders to take control. We will gain respect and prestige with a wife born of a village."

Rarely did Anders use his ultimate authority as leader of their triad, but he was set to do so now. "We are in no position to seek status as village elders. As for controlling a wife, we are claiming a mate, not a servant. I will not support your ridiculous position."

"The numbers are not in your favor, my friend," Johan sneered.

As soon as Jemina came into view later that day, Anders was smitten. Everything about her thrilled him, from the way she walked, to the gentle swells of her slender frame. He longed to expose the pale skin covered by the warrior cloak she wore, and run his face along each inch, inhaling her scent and tasting her essence. He grew hard just imagining the treasures he would unveil. He would gladly give up the promise of a city bride for the mere chance to win this beauty's hand.

She graced him with a smile as her fathers introduced her and explained details of the competition. Hendrix and Johan barely listened to the older men, instead pressing the new set of fledglings from their village for information about the visitors from Urijah. Shaking his head, Anders listened attentively to her guardians. He would fill his triad in on what was expected when the time came. There was no doubt in his mind now. He would abandon the city bride whom they could rightfully claim in the morning, for a chance to win Jemina as a wife.

All too soon, Jemina and her fathers departed, giving the Village of Finn time to prepare for the morning ceremony. Anders sought out his triad so they could approach Enoch, the Finn elder present, as one to request leave of their position. He found them talking to the elder. The elder's stance was stiff. He was troubled by what was being said. Anders cursed, wishing his foolish triad had waited for him before discussing departing the city wall. He would have found a way to get Enoch to see the logic in such a bold move. But Hendrix and Johan had already wreaked havoc on the situation. It was up to him to smooth things over again.

His impulsive triad departed as Anders reached where the elder stood. One glance at the old man's face told Anders that Hendrix and Johan had found a way to insult rules and traditions yet again. "Did they tell you of their plans?" the elder bluntly asked.

"They have, and before you reject the notion, there are sound reasons for this path." At least my reasoning is logical, Anders wanted to add, but did not.

"You support their odd decision?" The elder was clearly shocked. "Maybe I should not be so surprised. You never wanted to be paired with them in the first place, yet you put aside your wishes when your village leaders prevailed on you to do so."

So his triad did not realize Anders was now willing to depart the wall with them and seek Jemina's hand in marriage? Rarely did he get to outwit the pair. He would savor this small victory for a few days. "After meeting Jemina, I am determined to win any competition necessary to have her as a mate."

The old man was flustered by the declaration. "But without a triad, how do you hope to participate?"

Being in the dark about anything displeased Anders. He tensed and waited for the elder to explain further. "I told Hendrix and Johan it was foolish to give up on a sure bride in hopes of one whom they might not win. But replacing you with Crosby, no matter how much the village bride seemed to be taken with him was ridiculous indeed. Women appear to only see his attractive face and forget his lack of skills as a warrior. Did you hear of the lioness that attacked us en route here? Crosby was inches from the village bride, a sword at his side, but clueless of the danger. Had it not been for the others in his triad, she could have been fatally wounded. I explained as much to Hendrix and Johan, but they were unperturbed. They are determined to give up their best warrior to take on an inept one."

Realization eventually poured on Anders like a cool, winter shower. As it washed down his body, so did his resolve. His triad had cast him aside without a second thought, not even bothering to tell him about the slight, but going straight to the elder. Nodding slowly, he planned his own path, no longer burdened by the two traitors he had worked so hard to help.

If he stayed here, he would be allowed to choose his own city bride without having to confer with two other grooms. Yet the idea held little appeal to him. Jemina was a gift too valuable to leave unprotected. Without a triad, he could never win her hand in marriage. But he could work to ensure she did not get bonded to the monsters he used to call brothers. He would protect her from that fate even at the cost of his own future.

EACH WARRIOR MOVED with caution knowing multiple strangers were within attacking distance. Hands on weapons, they circled around one another under the cover of green, thick foliage. Aras did not normally travel alone, knowing evildoers sought such easy targets. A solitary man shifting through these parts was easy to subdue, no matter how well he wielded his sword.

To his right, one stranger hid. This adversary was cunning, only moving when Aras did, thus masking the sounds of his own course. At the right, a bold warrior moved, letting anyone around know he considered himself superior and dared anyone to try attacking him. Something about the tactic was familiar to him, and Aras considered carefully before trusting his gut.

"Loinbard, if you are the person moving about, know two things. First, a third warrior moves less than ten feet from your current position. Second, when we were children, I always bested you. Now is not the time to test your skill against me."

"Don't put away your weapon but be careful not to swing it in my direction," his brother's deep voice ordered. He eased out from behind a large oak tree, his eyes staring in the direction of the third warrior hiding somewhere in the distance. "Why aren't you at the wall, brother, working to earn yourself a city bride who will steal your heart and your daughters?"

Aras' eyes narrowed, but he did not lessen his sense of alertness. "Must you speak so freely about such matters?" So many questions needed to be addressed. What was his younger sibling doing this far from their village? Why was he venturing off alone? How were they going to deal with the third person hiding close by?

"We are in private," Loinbard announced loudly, "or we will be soon, after we kill the evildoer trying to sneak up on us." Again, Aras took exception to his brother's rash words. He turned to glare him into silence.

"No evildoer is about," a third man replied. "Just one warrior from the Village of Finn and two loud and unseasoned fledglings from the Village of Konrad, if your accents are to be trusted."

"Unseasoned, indeed!" Loinbard put aside his weapon and flexed his muscles. "Show yourself. Let us judge for ourselves if you are friend or enemy."

Sword held high; the third man slowly revealed himself. From the muted colors of browns and grays on his loincloth, Aras recognized him as a warrior fresh from the wall of the city where the Finn soldiers guarded. "You are going to the Village of Urijah to compete for the bride there?" Sheathing his own sword, he cursed his luck. How many men would he have to fight for the chance to wed the enchanting Jemina?

"You, too?" Both Loinbard and the stranger answered together.

Satisfied there was no threat to eliminate, Anders dropped his own weapon. "Brothers?" Aras nodded. "Where is the third member of your triad?"

"There is no third member," Aras announced. His brother gave him a puzzled scan. "Jasper and Border refused to join me in this quest. They didn't share my feelings about wanting to vie for a village bride."

"And your triad?" Anders asked, his eyes locked on Loinbard.

"Until now, I have avoided joining one. Another group from our village is making their way to the Village of Urijah. They were not keen on accepting me as a fourth member of their team. I am hoping they will have a change of mind when I show up and proclaim my determination to win the competition. Have you misplaced your own triad?"

Anders eyes grew cold. "They replaced me with another before venturing to Urijah. I have no wish to rejoin their number anyway, but I will be announcing my intention to win the strong willed Jemina, if only to protect her from the fools who underestimated my resolve."

"None of us have a chance," Aras stated the obvious. "Her fathers will probably dismiss us as contenders outright, and we won't even get a chance to move past the village border. I would not allow my daughter to marry a single husband, knowing he would leave her alone in a strange village if he were killed in battle."

"There is one way around this matter," Loinbard suggested, gaining their attention. "I swore I would never speak such blasphemy, yet here I am doing just that. Shall we form a triad and work as a team to claim a bride?"

"There are many issues with your plan, brother." Aras shook his head. "Our new friend here is not of our village. Our green and black colors tend to clash with Finn attire. Someone is bound to notice."

"I don't know how things are in the Village of Konrad, but triads work cycles together, learning to move as one, bond as a team and build their tactics. Currently, I don't know your brother's name and neither of you know mine. We are just a few hours from the village where Jemina's suitors are gathering. How do you propose we cram all those skills in such a brief journey?"

"The alternative means not even being allowed inside the village boundaries to even participate," Loinbard announced. "I suggest we walk slowly but talk fast."

"My name is Aras. If we form this alliance, how would it be determined which of our villages we would live in with our new bride?"

"They call me Anders. If we were to form a triad, I am amendable to dwelling in the Village of Konrad, but only if I may bring my mother and three younger brothers with me. My fathers all perished in a clash with the evildoers who attacked our village four cycles ago. I am now the oldest of my family unit. It falls to me to care for them."

"It is little price to pay for having your cooperation." Loinbard glanced at Aras, waiting for his next challenge.

"How many cycles are you, Anders? I was not the senior member of my last triad. I found it difficult to be led by someone who had different goals from myself." Aras was not shy about proclaiming his gravest concern in forming a new triad.

"I am twenty-one cycles old," he replied but quickly followed up the comment, "I was the leader in my last triad and found it frustrating to try guiding people who did not want to work as a team. Since we would be moving to your village, it only makes sense for you to be our leader. But beware. I will offer my opinion and voice any concerns I have if I believe you try to lead us in an unethical manner. I don't care if you have dreams of becoming a powerful leader one day. I will no longer bend my code of honor to pursue a goal I do not believe in."

Aras wondered at sharing the private secret he sheltered for many cycles. If he were to join with this man, there should be no secrets for they would be as good as family from this point on.

They needed to trust one another completely if they were to function as a team. He silently asked the Creator to guide him. A white dove suddenly landed on a nearby branch. Its feathers were flawless as it perched there, ruffling its wings. Without warning an arrow flew from the right and the bird dropped lifeless to the ground.

Motioning for Loinbard to move to his right and Anders to go left, Aras slipped into the foliage and waited. A young boy, no more than fifteen cycles at best, emerged from the trees to collect the bird. Another boy scampered after him. "Why'd you have to kill it?" the second boy whined. He looked no more than six cycles.

"Because we can't feed our family with live doves, fool," the older boy raged. From their tattered clothes, Aras knew they were offspring of evildoers. His heart lurched at the slight pitiful, skinny frames of the boys. Life outside the walls of the villages and city was brutal. He would have tried to take the youths back with him when he returned home, but the village elders would no doubt turn them away. It was bad enough he was going to claim a warrior from Finn as a member of his triad. The last thought came too natural to him, Aras knew he had his answer from the Creator on the rightness of forming this new triad.

Once the young boys were gone, Aras, Loinbard and Anders stepped out into the clearing again. "We have much to learn about one another, Anders from the village of Finn. Might I suggest we take my brother's suggestion? Shall we walk slowly and talk fast?" The three shook hands and started on their way, first sharing information about their training as warriors, then their thoughts on managing a family unit, and finally their opinions about how best to go about winning Jemina as a bride.

5

Proclaiming their Desire

Most of the people from the Village of Urijah gathered in the meeting area, anxiously awaiting the beginning of the ceremony, which celebrated the end of one cycle and the birth of another. Her fathers had not arrived as of yet. They were no doubt reviewing the triads seeking to be allowed past the boundaries of their land. Jemina had always planned to join them, advising them on which suitors to welcome and which to send away. But she cared not about the task now.

All three of the men she had dreamed of wedding were disqualified from seeking her. The perfect lovers she envisioned weren't even a triad at all. She had met them each separately and learned how poorly suited they were as husbands. Aras, though strong and proud, was also too opinionated for her. Loinbard could stir her passions, but she only stoked his own desire due to her position as a village born bride. Most disappointing of all was Crosby. No matter how attractive he might be, he did not have the skill of a real warrior. Aye, she could protect herself if needed, but it was necessary to have a husband who could aid in keeping their family unit safe.

Alistrair made a production of entering the center platform. The other elders came to sit in the front rows circling the area. A brief smile touched her lips as Jael and his triad approached, their new bride donning her bridal dress, a decorative hood blocking all but the slightest hint of a pale profile. Her twin had finally returned from his duty at the wall. Soon the city bride his triad had claimed would be introduced to their people, welcomed as a new citizen of Urijah.

Her mother waved from her position near the front. Her fathers' seats were still empty. Behind them, three sets of three vacant chairs awaited. If tradition played out as it should, soon three triads would come forward and join the gathering. When the time came, and her name was offered up as an available bride, each set of men would be allowed to speak about their worthiness to compete for Jemina's hand in marriage. For cycles now, she had eagerly awaited this very night, but now she dreaded what was to follow.

A trumpet sounded in the distance, a sign that strangers were walking freely among the village. Though elders welcomed suitors, villages were cautious enough to be on guard whenever outsiders were present. Enoch nodded with approval as Jemina's fathers ushered three triads to their assigned seats. Everyone in attendance strained to have a look at the contenders, but not the future bride. She would not get her hopes up again by favoring one group over another. The Creator would likely snatch away her choice as a lesson in being too proud.

"Another cycle has passed, fellow descendants of Urijah, and we have experienced countless losses and gains." Alistrair wore a flowing robe of black and blue, his usual unkempt hair, combed into submission for the ceremony. "As is our habit, let us reflect on what has brought us to this point in time, a cluster of survivors from a world gone mad more than a century before.

"Old earth must have been a glorious sight to behold. We

have all heard tales of the wondrous inventions that made life so easy back then. They did not need to keep fires burning, hunt for meat or work long hours tilling the soil. A flip of a switch and light flooded an entire hall. Places were set aside for them to browse through food items nicely packaged and ready to cook. Most astounding of all, if a family unit did not feel like working to prepare a meal, they simply went to a business which concocted the food and served it to them at fancy tables lined with extravagant linens and utensils." Patting his extending belly, Alistrair chuckled. "Oh, to have lived in such glorious times.

"Such inventions freed citizens to pursue other activities. Some worked to find cures for diseases or ways to improve life even more. But many used their time to seek power, money and Creator-like status. Wars broke out on all of earth, and death was widespread thanks to machines developed to make murdering an easier task too.

"Konrad, Finn and our founding father Urijah managed to survive, as did their loved ones and friends. Each set out to rebuild what old earth had destroyed. Strife lived on, unfortunately. Some of the survivors still harbored evil desires and needed to be driven out of established villages. Weapons, once deemed unnecessary, had to be created to keep evildoers from destroying the good that had finally been reestablished.

"A group of citizens from each village objected to using force to maintain a lawful system. They left our number to establish their own city. Their steadfast resolve to avoid conflict eventually faded as cycles passed. The city leaders ultimately needed to contact the village elders and worked out a treaty that fulfilled the greatest needs of our residents and city populaces. We agreed to send some of our skilled warriors to protect their wall, and they gift us with a bride each cycle to help ensure our numbers do not fall too low."

Jemina blew a strand of hair out of her face and rested her

chin on the palm of one propped up arm. Alistrair's voice droned on and on. He spoke of the births and deaths of villagers, listing all major events from the start of last cycle to now. Two babies had been snatched from the birthing section of the healer's compound. The armed warriors stationed around the building were powerless to prevent the unseen evil that stole the babes as their mothers slept from the exhausting duty of childbirth. "We will not stop searching for the sources of this evil crime. Those responsible will pay dearly."

Alistrair finally moved to happier topics, asking several family units to stand and hold aloft infants of varying ages. Many sons had been born during the closing cycle. Jemina hoped he would dedicate a long time on offering his blessings upon each child. His long windedness meant stalling the part of the ceremony she feared most. Fidgeting with her own dress, she picked at one of the delicate designs her mother had carefully stitched at the wrist.

Had she wanted; she would have worn the heirloom dress Jael's bride now had on. As a village bride, she had first right of refusal since this was her blessed day as coming of age. If she thought her dream husbands would see her in it, she might have selfishly chosen to claim the right of appearing in it. But Jemina no longer looked forward to this ceremony or the competition to follow. Let her new sister-in-law savor the memory.

Jael and his triad eventually stepped on the platform; their cloaked bride carefully rose to stand on a small plateau for all to see. Each man took turns saying kind words about the woman they had claimed from the city. Jemina was proud of her brother's speech.

He shared the same red hair, but his was always groomed. Freckles ran across his nose and his steel-blue eyes were full of control and wisdom even with his young age. "Often I have dreamed of the woman I would one day be privileged to wed. I hoped, when the time came to select from the city's offerings, that the Creator would help my triad see past physical beauty to choose a worthy wife and mother to run our family unit."

He paused a moment, then glanced up at his bride, pulling the hood from her head. An approving round of applause scattered across the audience. Blonde hair framed a lovely, innocent face. Her emerald eyes were large and glistening as if his words had pleased her. "The moment our dear Giannis exited the final wall of the city, I knew my prayers had been answered. I know not how the other women looked, for I only had eyes for this angel. It was as if the perfect woman I had imagined claiming for countless cycles had somehow managed to step out of my dreams and into my heart. Chaim and Moshe obviously agree. Alistrair himself approved of the selection and our vows were delivered immediately. We are blessed to call her wife."

Jemina allowed herself to be jealous of her new sister-in-law for a moment or two. What would it be like to have three men stand before the Creator and village to proclaim her worth? Oh, being a village bride made Jemina a jewel, but she wanted to be recognized for her inner traits, not her place of birth.

Then she noticed the expression on Giannis' face. The poor girl was shaking, clearly ill at ease with being gawked at by so many strangers. Jemina had heard rumors that city brides were unaware they would be offered up as payment for a village's protection at the wall, and supplies of fuel and meat. If such was true, Jael's bride was no doubt terrified of all the upheaval taking place around her. How horrible it must be, to be pulled away from life as you know it, and thrust into a village of outsiders, an existence foreign to all you understand?

Jemina was determined to befriend the girl and help her adjust. She knew her brother and his triad would do their best to help the city bride feel welcomed, but sometimes it took one frightened bride to understand the uncertainties of another.

Without warning Jemina realized all eyes were on her. Alistrair was gesturing for her to join him on the platform. Her fathers were already at the elder's side, her mother beaming next to them. The elder's loud voice hushed the crowd. "The beginning of this cycle marks a monumental event. I believe Ellias has an important announcement to make concerning his family unit."

Ellias waited until Ellena, Darnish and Leodon gave him approving nods before speaking. "Our family is twice blessed. Our oldest son and his triad have brought home a lovely bride. May they gift us with many grandchildren to spoil." He paused to allow the clapping to subside. "We have put off making this next announcement for as long as possible, waiting a few years past the customary age of seventeen cycles, but the time has finally arrived. It is with honor, and a good bit of sadness, that we proclaim our beautiful daughter, Jemina is ready to become a bride herself."

The crowd gained their feet and cheered deafeningly. "Long live the descendants of Urijah," they chanted in unison over and over again until Alistrair motioned for them to regain their seats.

Darnish spoke next. "The official announcement of her availability was spread through the neighboring villages. We traveled to the walls of the city at both the regions patrolled by Konrad and that of Finn as well. All interested suitors were instructed to present themselves for consideration to compete for Jemina's hand in marriage by this date."

Leodon's voice cracked as he started to speak, and he took a moment to regain his composure. His wife Ellena held his hand to lend him some of her strength. "Our triad has been busy since returning from making this announcement. No less than ten sets of warriors appeared at our border in hopes of being allowed inside."

Gulping, Jemina marveled at the news. Ten groups? Thirty men were interested in seeking her as their bride? She was awestruck more by that fact, than seeing her generally emotionless father, Leodon being close to breaking down before witnesses.

Alistrair spoke, no doubt to give the fathers a chance to gain their composure. "Thirty outsiders running amok in our village?" he quipped, giving a mock shudder. "Thank the Creator, we had the wisdom to limit the number of triads allowed to compete."

Ellias spoke again, saving Leodon from the task. "After speaking with each group, listening to their reasons for seeking the pleasure of wedding our daughter, and discussing in great detail how they would care for her and the children she blessed their village with, we selected three of the worthiest triads. Please help us in welcoming them. Would the triad from Finn please rise and state your intention to our citizens?"

Jemina could not believe her eyes when she saw Crosby among the strange men who stood up. The other members of his triad were not at his side. Instead a harsh looking man with small eyes stood beside him. Another man boldly regarded those around him with a slight sneer, as if he was judging their value and found it questionable. The beady-eyed man spoke in a loud, clear voice. "I am Hendrix. My brother Johan and friend Crosby and I seek to prove our superiority by competing for the beautiful Jemina. Having her as our bride would be an honor and the Village of Finn would do all in its power to make her feel at home."

Jemina felt her skin crawl. While she could stomach spending her life lying beside the attractive Crosby, despite his uselessness in battle, she did not trust the man named Hendrix. Something about him made her uncomfortable. His announcement did little to soothe her concern. He spoke of being superior, winning her as an honor and his village making her feel welcome. She was but a trophy his triad hoped to bring home.

Darnish stepped forward and spoke after the Finn triad finally sat down. "Would the triad from Konrad please rise and state your intentions to our citizens?"

A cluster of three men stepped into the light, and Jemina felt a bit more at ease at the sight of them. They were younger than the men from Finn, probably fledglings new to the wall of the city or a set ready to start their duty there.

A dark man with rich brown curls and scruffy whiskers acted as spokesman for the group. "Thank you for allowing us entrance to your village. I am Tyler. My blood brothers Sage and Riley joined me in the journey here to your impressive community in hopes of seeking the honor of competing for your beautiful village daughter. We served the city for one cycle, but decided to forgo our second year there in hopes of winning Jemina's hand in marriage. We promise, should we prove ourselves worthy of winning the competition, to spend the rest of our lives protecting the precious gift your village offers."

Ellena smiled brightly at the warriors from Konrad. Her approval gave Jemina hope. Her mother, along with her fathers, would come up with the challenges each triad faced. Ellena would find a way to make sure Jemina wed the best group of men.

Leodon found his voice when the Konrad group sat down. "It is challenging to announce the final triad. This third group of men chosen to compete is unlike any other triad we have ever encountered or even heard of existing. I believe a short explanation is necessary before I ask them to stand. Three individual men chose to travel here alone, in hopes to be considered, though each had no triad to represent him." Even the elders turned to stare at the third set of men. The crowd was eager for more news. Jemina stood in the very center of the platform, and light from torches made seeing into the crowd difficult. She squinted her eyes to no avail.

"As they made the journey, the three men chanced upon one another. Two of the three were blood brothers from the Village of Konrad, who had not aligned themselves in the past, each taking a different path in life. The third man comes from the

Village of Finn. He was once a member of Hendrix and Johan's triad, but was replaced by Crosby at the last minute. Since he had already decided to try for Jemina's hand, this Finn warrior gave up the right to select a city bride this very day to travel to our home, knowing he would likely not even make it past the village border.

"The individual warriors continued their journey here, discussing their intent to seek our daughter's hand, and bonding in a common goal decided to become a new triad. Their remarkable tale intrigued us, and their determination pleased Ellias, Darnish and me. We also knew, if our wife heard of their grit, and we failed to allow them to compete, Ellena would have kicked us out of her bed for cycles to come." Laughter erupted, those present shocked at the generally solemn man's gibe. Ellena playfully slapped his arm, but Leodon's somber demeanor returned. His voice was strong now. "Would the new triad of Konrad and Finn please rise and state your intent to our citizens?"

Jemina gasped when their faces finally came into view. She blinked a few times, to make sure she was not dreaming. Aras, the warrior from the wall stood there, his bleached hair tucked behind his ears. Beside him was the Konrad flirt called Loinbard, his piercing sky-blue eyes locking on hers before he dared to give her a playful wink. Studying the third man, Jemina was shocked to find his long, thick hair clasped tightly behind his head in a leather strap. His lips were hidden behind a full beard and groomed mustache, but she could almost feel them tasting various parts of her body.

As she had suspected last night, Crosby wasn't the third man from her dreams. She had been naïve to think he was, for her dream lover was strong and attentive, not self-absorbed and useless. The Creator had not abandoned her as she had feared. The three men he filled her dreams with did exist, a perfect triad, one formed for the sole intent of winning her hand in marriage. A smile filled her face as she listened to the men speak.

"Our villages of Konrad and Finn would surely be pleased to know you accepted us within your number. They would likely be surprised, too, as none of this could have been foreseen. The unlikely forming of our unique triad will come as a shock to them when we return, but I know the rightness of our union will cast aside any objections the elders might have. I am Aras. This is my blood brother Loinbard. We hail from the village of Konrad.

"I chose to represent our village at the city walls, as was my duty as a first-born son. Loinbard was determined to pursue the rarest of opportunities, the chance to compete for a village born bride. Forming a triad was out of the question given such different quests. But the Creator had his own plans and our paths crossed on our journey here.

"I am pleased to announce I have a new brother named Anders from the Village of Finn. After seeing Jemina's beauty and watching the grace she moved with, he was compelled to seek her as his wife, also. As Jemina's father stated, we individually set off with the desire to seek her hand in marriage. Joined by our common goal, we comprehended the natural solution of forming a unique triad. For what is a triad, if not for the purpose of earning the right to love and protect a wife. Know this, Village of Urijah. If we are blessed to wed your village bride, we will take her back to the Village of Konrad, where she will be treated as the rare gem she is.

"You all, no doubt, are wondering how our living arrangement will work, since our triad originates from two different regions. My new brother Anders has agreed to relocate to our village, as well as the remaining members of his family unit. He would retain his citizenship as a member of the Finn line, but also be considered an honorary Konrad, too.

"His fathers gave their lives to protect their village from evil-doers challenging their border during a recent battle. Anders is duty bound to take care of his mother and younger brothers. As his new triad, we accept this responsibility as our own, too. Know that we are honest, hardworking warriors who do not take our duty to our village or family lightly. If we succeed in claiming Jemina's hand, every one of you can rest assured that she will be well cared for all her living days. The earlier chant you gave would be fulfilled. 'Long live the descendants of Urijah, Konrad and Finn'."

6

Breaking Bread

The traditional meal shared after the ceremony found Aras, Loinbard and Anders sitting at a long table, far from the woman they hoped to wed. The moment the Elder Alistrair instructed them on where Jemina and her family would take their meal, Hendrix and Johan shoved Crosby forward, assuring they might locate the best position to claim their chairs. The other triad from Konrad shook their heads in disgust, but waited, as did Aras' triad, for Jemina and her immediate family to take their seats before approaching the area.

Jael, Jemina's twin, and his triad ushered their new bride to the head of the same wooden table. Other strangers sat nearby, no doubt from Chaim and Moshe's families. Next to them, Ellias, Darnish and Leodon pulled up some chairs. Jemina sat, and left a spot for her mother. The Finn warriors sat directly across from her, but Hendrix pointed for Crosby to go and claim the chair meant for her mother.

Ellena did not notice at first because she had made it her duty to personally prepare Giannis' plate. She gave her new daughter-in-law a tight hug before asking her mate Ellias to give the blessing before they ate. Only then did Ellena realize her position had been adjusted. Instead of being forced to sit separate from her husbands, she sat on Darnish's lap for the meal.

Aras smiled, imagining his own second mother Attie would have done the same. Jemina got her free spirit from her lovely mother, along with her wondrous red hair. As the older man offered a blessing to the Creator, Aras' mind wandered back to the time when his father Ryder had forced him and his younger brothers to sit at the table when his triad brought their city bride back to their village. He grimaced, recalling the rude way he had behaved that night, his rebellious teenage hormones making him act foolish and unkind.

He glanced sideways at Loinbard and noticed his brother seemed to be reliving uncomfortable memories, too. Thank goodness, their second mother Attie had forgiven them. Their family unit had grown strong through the cycles that followed. They clung to one another during tragic times, and made plans to avenge wrongs forced upon them.

The newlywed triad was painfully attentive to their wife, Aras noted. Jael, who bore a strong resemblance to Jemina, hand fed his bride. It was clear he already had strong emotions where the girl was concerned, despite only knowing her for a few hours. Had he really dreamed of her before this day, the flesh and blood woman whom his triad claimed? Jael had claimed it was as if his dreams had become real.

The Konrad warrior had never allowed himself such luxuries as dreaming of a future wife. He dreaded claiming a bride, giving her his love and devotion, and knowing he could lose her and the children she bore him because of a horrible sin perpetrated by the leaders of city. Not just the city, he reminded himself. The village healers were just as culpable. Hatred filled his heart as Aras watched those around him, trying to surmise which woman might hold such a role here. The lighting was too weak to allow focusing on tables more than one or two away.

"Notice how my brother cannot stop touching his wife?"

Jemina's silvery tone brought Aras' attention back to his immediate surroundings. Was he mistaken, or was she speaking directly toward his triad? His second mother, Attie, often made odd comments like this. After observing his fathers' reactions for many cycles, he gleaned she was instructing her mates on the ways to please her without directly ordering them around.

Was the beautiful Jemina employing the same technique now? It would be nice to have a wife who helped her mates understand her wants and needs. Having to guess at such matters would be impossible and frustrating for all involved. If only Jemina was in arm's reach, he could show her his appreciation of her hints by feeding her as her brother fed his bride.

Crosby, who Aras had assumed to be a total nitwit, with not a clue or desire to please anyone but himself, seemed to figure out what Jemina was suggesting much faster than Aras had. The Konrad warrior's gut clenched, as did his fists, as the Finn warrior started stroking her arm and popping bits of juicy fruit in her mouth. When a small bit of juice trickled down her chin, he used a finger to wipe it off before bringing it to his mouth.

"I hope the challenges we face involve hand to hand combat," Aras muttered. "It would give me great pleasure to crush that ass' hand and sever that finger, before breaking every bone I can reach."

"You'd do better to wound Hendrix," Anders quietly suggested, eating his meal without looking up. "The foolish boy they replaced me with is only following his new triad's bidding. The moment Jemina made her statement, I saw Hendrix nudge Crosby with his foot and gesture for him to hand feed her. Crosby doesn't have an original thought in his head. He is only a tool being used by his triad to better position themselves in the competition. The moment he is no longer an asset, they will dispose of him as they did me."

"Would they do the same to Jemina?" Aras felt outraged.

"Without hesitation." Anders made a show of concentrating

on the food in his plate, not wanting to show the disgust in his eyes. "Even if we do not win her hand, we must make sure Hendrix and Johan never claim Jemina as their wife."

"Agreed," Loinbard uttered, and Aras found his sibling to be just as passionate about his dislike of the Finn triad. His blood brother offered his opinion in a grave tone. "When the time for battle comes, I hope I come up against the third member of their little team. Johan. What a plain name for someone who appears to think he is so superior to everyone else. If he flexes his muscles at Jemina one more time, I might have to slam his ugly face into the table."

A member of the other Konrad triad tried to start up a conversation. His name was Sage, Aras recalled. "We have much to learn about Jemina and only a short time to do so. Would you tell us about your daughter? What was she like as a child? Has she always been so delightful?" His question was put to her fathers, yet he smiled directly at Jemina. Aras wanted to slam his fist into the boy's face so he could remove the foul expression.

Instead, he nudged his brother roughly, demanding to know why he had not been smart enough to consider such a brilliant strategy. The more they learned about Jemina, the better equipped they would be to win her hand and please her as potential mates. He listened carefully, indicating with a nod for Anders and Loinbard to do the same.

Her fathers appeared at a loss of what to share, so their wife addressed the question instead. "Jemina has always been full of delightful surprises. In fact, from the very start of her life, she has been amazing us. I labored for hours to bring Jael forth. He was my first-born and a very challenging delivery. Our little princess followed him out without a smidgen of warning. We did not realize I was carrying two babes. One-minute Dalia, she's our village healer, was catching Jael, and the next, she was dropping him on my belly and guiding his sister out."

Ellena smiled at the triads as she talked. If Jemina aged as well as her mother, her lucky husbands would be truly blessed, Aras decided.

"She's been following along after me ever since," Jael announced. "I swear, she might have tried to go off and join my triad when we left to protect the city walls if Alistrair wouldn't have found the strength to deny her plea."

"A woman at the wall?" Hendrix sounded appalled. "Even cast-offs are considered too valuable to be allowed to be stationed there."

"Having a few cast-offs available might have helped pass the time as we patrolled those boring bits of land between the walls," Johan said aloud, earning himself a disapproving glare from Ellena and a swift kick under the table from Hendrix. "Only as a means to better prepare ourselves in the ways of pleasing a new bride, of course. Cast-offs serve a useful purpose, though I am sure coupling with a wife would be just as enjoyable." His attempt at saving face fell flat.

Leodon pushed back his chair and started to gain his feet, when Ellias opted to change the direction the discussion was heading. "I believe the most important thing any triad winning our daughter's hand in marriage needs to know is that our Jemina is an accomplished warrior in her own right. Tis the truth, her command of the sword is equal to, if not superior to many of the fledglings she and her brother trained alongside."

Tyler, the leader from the Konrad triad, let out a loud peel of laughter, assuming the older man was jesting. As soon as he realized it was not a joke, the embarrassed warrior made a production of reaching for his glass and swallowing a large portion of wine. His pink face gave his mortification away.

Unfortunately for Aras, Tyler was seated just to his left. Jemina glowered at him instead of the younger warrior, no doubt recalling his unwise comments from their first meeting at the wall. Adjusting the neckline on the shirt he wore, Aras remembered he had dared to mock her size and potential skill as a warrior. He started to defend himself, but realized he would sound even more foolish trying to blame another. He would have to accept responsibility for this rudeness, his fault or not, because of a foolish error he made in the past. Would he ever learn to hold his tongue and think before speaking? From Attie to Jemina, his harsh words often pained those he cared about. Well, Aras understood he no doubt said things other men in his life took exception to, but he really did not care about their trivial feelings.

Anders tried to draw attention away from Aras. "I am glad to learn you are a skilled warrior, Jemina. My own mother had to protect my younger siblings after evildoers breached our border, slaughtered my fathers and tried to penetrate our family unit. She had no formal training in the manner of wielding a sword. I believe her natural instincts as a mother provided her with the necessary skills when the time came. She avenged my fathers' deaths, killing four of the five men who had attacked before other warriors from our village managed to come to her aid."

Jemina sat up tall, her eyes glued to Anders. Aras noted the admiration in her eyes and tucked this insight away into a corner of his mind. Knowledge was power. His little village daughter respected those who protected their own and did not cower in the face of danger. His thoughts were confirmed when she spoke. "Your mother is a remarkable woman, sir. I would be honored to meet her one day so I can learn more about her courage."

"Such is the irony, sweet Jemina. To lay eyes on my dear mother, you might consider her to be meek. She is a tiny thing in stature and weight, but her inner strength takes over if the need arises," Anders said. "If the Creator does one day bless me with any daughters, I will see to it they can defend themselves and others if the need arises."

"All women should be instructed in such matters." The comment came from the person least likely to say such a thing.

All eyes turned to rest on the small figure of the city bride who sat at the head of the table. Clad in a white, carefully designed bridal gown, she had not uttered a sound until now, and most who saw her were inclined to think she was too overwhelmed to speak. Her voice was steady and full of passion as she spoke, though. Jael rested a protective arm around her shoulders as she continued.

"Where I come from, defending yourself or those you care about is considered wrong. I watched someone I grew up with endure cycles of horrible taunts and vicious insults by older, hateful kids. Ignore them, she was told when she asked the elders to protect her. Turn their ugly words into a means to strengthen your inner resolve, they suggested." Giannis laughed bitterly.

"Once, when I was ten cycles old, I found the courage to stand up to the others who taunted her, demanding they cease their cruelty or face the consequences. The city priestess heard my angry promises, and I was sanctioned for being confrontational. It was not my concern that the poor girl was being teased, I was told. I needed to concern myself with making our city a better place for the whole, not try to improve the life of an individual."

Her emerald eyes grew dark as she continued her telling. "The true offenders went unpunished, and soon increased their mocking of my friend knowing it angered me and hurt her. The stress wore down her self-worth, and eventually she threw herself off of the tallest roof in the city. I will never forget the day it happened. I raged at the city priestess who led our region. Bella's death was her fault and I swore I would find a way to escape the city one day."

"It would please me to teach you the ways of defending yourself, wife," Jael told her. Her mates Chaim and Moshe agreed to instruct her as well.

"And I will help you master the way to thrust a dagger and how to swing a sword with precision," Jemina declared. "You and I are sisters now, Giannis. I may soon be leaving this village after I become a bride, but I know you will remain behind, championing the cause of our women, and their right to be allowed to train for whatever path they choose in life." Raising a goblet of wine high in the air, she offered a toast. "Long live the descendants of Urijah, be they women or men!"

Aras shook his head, not in sanction, but in weary acceptance. If he managed to win Jemina's hand in marriage, he would likely spend his life chasing after willful children who were ready to challenge long held traditions. He took comfort in knowing his little warriors would be an asset when the time came to avenge the wrongs of the city.

Aras wished he could find a way to spend time with Giannis. She had a wealth of information about the inner workings of the city and no loyalty to rulers who were unfair. He needed to gather all the facts he could about what went on behind the inner wall. Who was in charge? What was the general layout of the land? Where were the women inside the city allowed to travel? Every bit of knowledge put his family one step closer to righting a wrong.

7

Views on Scolding

A blaring horn sounded, rousing the sleeping warriors who occupied the center of the village of Urijah. Aras and his triad leaped from their sleeping rolls, instantly alert for potential danger, weapons ready to strike. The other Konrad triad also bounded to their feet, ready to do battle. A few feet away, slumbering peacefully in the middle of the platform where Jemina and her family stood the night before, Crosby turned to his side, his blond locks shielding the rising sun from his view, unaware of the commotion. Hendrix and Johan had managed to finally gain their feet but each had to search for their swords. They had made no obvious effort to stow the weapons close by before falling asleep.

"Good morning, potential brothers," a small child yelled at the top of his lungs before blowing deeply into his horn again. Aras was the first to realize all was safe and put down his weapon. The others followed his lead. Stretching and shaking off the last bits of sleep, the men started putting away their belongings.

While in the Village of Urijah, they would camp in the

center of the community. According to custom, they rested there because they were still fledglings awaiting the right to claim their bride. Instead of the city wall, they guarded the meeting area where their bride would come to wed the victors.

Aras, now a seasoned soldier knew the true reason. Outsiders were not trusted, even those welcomed within the grounds to compete for a village bride. While warriors took turns patrolling the border of Urijah, a more subtle lot, no doubt guarded this meeting area, guaranteeing all strangers were accounted for and not a threat to the village. Scanning the area, he noted no less than nine hardened, battle ready men observing them from behind trees and buildings.

The boy playing the horn suddenly stopped. Aras turned to find out why. Loinbard was sanctioning Hendrix, who had tired of the child's off-key tune, and apparently launched a hard shoe at the boy's head. His brother roared, "No honorable warrior would bring harm to a child. If you seek someone to spar with, by all means allow me to accommodate you."

One of the large soldiers who had been charged with keeping the triad from Finn in check had already begun advancing toward the platform. At first Aras thought it might even be the village elder called Alistrair, but dismissed the thought quickly. Someone of such high regard would not likely be playing wet nurse to visitors. Hearing Loinbard address the offending Hendrix must have soothed matters because Aras noticed the man melt back into the distance. No one had even noticed his presence except him. Aras had learned to be alert, to search for threats others did not even fear.

Hendrix sneered at those standing below him as he stood on the raised platform. The night before, as each triad selected a portion of land to set up camp, he and Johan had laid claim to the center. Neither of the other triads had even considered challenging for the position. They thought it disrespectful to sleep upon hallowed ground used to celebrate life and bring sad news of death.

The Finn warrior lifted his chin and sneered. "You speak bravely for a man of your position. We all heard about your past last night. You never even served a single cycle at the wall, fledgling. If your own village elders did not have enough faith in your fighting skills to send you there, why would I waste my time even conversing with the likes of you? Your blood is not worth spilling with my sword."

Anders put a hand on Loinbard's muscular shoulder, staying the younger man's movement forward. "Ironic how village elders decide which fledglings to send to the city walls, isn't it? Now that I have aligned myself with another village, I have learned many things. In Konrad, for instance, men are allowed to decide if they want to serve on the wall. Some, like my new brother here, train as warriors, and after proving their skill, go straight to guarding the village border because they don't seek a city bride."

His eyes had been on Hendrix as he spoke, but now Anders smiled at Loinbard before sharing more. "Now, in the village of Finn, things are somewhat different. All fledglings are expected to progress in their skills until they are deemed worthy to serve on the walls. If a man, or a pair of men in rare cases, fail to achieve such status, they may only go to the wall if they allow another, superior warrior to act as their leader." His tawny eyes flickered back to Hendrix again. "Even if this new leader is someone younger than them."

The boy with the horn started hooting with amusement. Picking up the shoe that had silenced him before, he tossed it back at the platform. "Our village has its own rules about who is allowed to go to the city wall," he called out. "Asses like those three would never be allowed to service the wall or the border. We value our safety too much."

A frustrated Leodon appeared from the west. "Finnigan,

what is taking you so long to make your announcement? The village cooks are ready to set the tables for the morning meal. Explain to the triads what you have been charged to say and head back home."

"Yes, Papa Leodon." The child's face reddened and his voice took on a monotone quality. "Honored guests of Urijah, please join us at our table for nourishment. During the meal, the first challenge for Jemina's hand will be detailed so you may prepare your triads accordingly." His father gone now that the duty had been taken care of, the boy smiled brightly at Anders, Loinbard and Aras.

"But you won't have much time to consider how to proceed," he spoke in hushed tones, repaying the triad's kindness with a bit of extra information. "The event takes place at the training fields at noon. Tis when the fledglings break for their meal so the area is available. My sister wields a wicked sword. Beware her left slash. It comes without warning and stings like the blazes."

"Is she going to slice us up and wait to see who survives to claim her as bride?" Anders mused with a tilted chin. "If so, Hendrix and Crosby will be the first to fall victim."

"Whatever the task, eat your meal quickly and meet me at the border so we can go into the forest to develop our tactics," Aras told his triad. The child called Finnigan was as spirited as his sister Jemina. It gave him hope. Their children might well be blessed with inner strength beyond measure. Would their son boast thick, untamed curls? His stepfather Wolf would be thrilled to have grandchildren with red hair. His second mother Attie often teased her mate about his preference for such hair but Aras had never figured out why.

JEMINA HEARD RILEY, one of the Konrad men, lean forward to

mock Aras. "We all would be alarmed at how intently our hopeful bride stares at you, my friend, fearing you had an unfair advantage over the rest of us. Yet one cannot help but notice she appears to be waiting to scold you for some slight you have given her."

"Village brides do not scold," she instructed those listening around her, as she carelessly began smearing a piece of bread with red jam. "We instruct, explain or challenge, but never scold. Until we are married, that is. Then we are free to scold as often as needed to help improve our mates' shortsightedness."

Finnigan began giggling, and Jemina give her youngest brother a sly wink. That brief moment of letting her focus on Aras waiver cost her. The element of surprise was on his side as he easily snatched the bread and knife from her hand. She groused at him as he started reapplying the jam in a methodical manner, leaving no speck on the top uncovered.

"Village husbands are much the same way," he said in a low, even tone. Others leaned in closer, trying to hear his words, but they were for her ears only. "We are free to scold as often as needed to help our mates learn any valuable lessons needed. I, myself, believe discussing issues is more productive than other means. But, if my wife were to do something foolish, say: put herself in danger, I would apply vast amounts of attention to her backside to help her learn the foolishness of her actions. I'd be careful not to bruise her flawless, pale skin, but hard enough to prompt long term effects."

"What did he say?" Gerald, another of Jemina's younger brothers demanded.

"He said he'd redden her arse if he were her husband," Finnigan hollered, and Jemina turned to shove him off of his chair.

For his part, Aras neither denied nor affirmed the child's account, infuriating her even more. His next warning was loud enough for all to hear. "I would be more cautious when scolding your younger brother, my lovely Jem. My blood brother Loinbard has taken a liking to the boy, acting as his champion of sorts. He has let it be known he will physically punish anyone doing harm to the child."

Her face turned crimson, but before she could reply, he turned away from her to address Anders. "How do the men in Finn 'scold' their mates? I am sure Jemina would be interested in learning as much as she could about those seeking her hand." The men started chuckling.

Jemina nearly fell from her chair as she stood up in frustration. "Enough!"

To think she had been rethinking the first challenge all during the morning meal, worried it was too harsh? Now she was determined to leave a lasting mark on each and every man seeking her hand in marriage. Jemina, village bride of Urijah, was not some timid wife they would lead around, telling her what she could and could not do. She was a warrior! It was time for them all to discover this fact. "Father, it is time to announce the first task."

Ellias pushed back his chair from the head of the table and waited for all eyes to lock on him before speaking. "There is still time," he glanced at Jemina one last time, but she crossed her arms in determination. "So be it. Triads, listen closely, for I have details of the first challenge you will face. Before explaining, I need to remind each of you of the rules for claiming a village daughter. First, challenges will be determined by the bride and her family, as many as necessary until a clear winner is named. Secondly, our family unit, namely Ellena, Darnish, Leodon and I will determine the winner of each challenge. Outsiders, Jemina or even our village elders cannot overturn our decision, so be warned. Arguing will not be tolerated."

Jemina wanted to slam her fist down on the table when her father's eyes lingered in her direction after he gave the caution. Was everyone resolved to humiliate her today? "I believe you were on your third point, father." The words came out through clenched teeth.

"Third, a winner will be declared once one triad wins three challenges. The losing triads will be allowed a few moments to collect their belongings before they are ushered off the village grounds. Finally, the joining ceremony will be held in the gathering area. Once the three nights of claiming are complete, we will rejoice with the new family unit at a celebration gathering before our strongest warriors help escort Jemina and her husbands to her new village." His voice faltered toward the end, but his wife came to stand beside him, tucking herself under his protective shoulder.

"May I explain the first challenge, husband?" He nodded, pleased she was sparing him from speaking while emotion weakened him. "A village bride is allowed to plan for one of the first three challenges. The elders felt it wise to give the girl being pursued a chance to put the odds in favor of any suitors she preferred. Most girls wait until the third challenge, allowing themselves to spend time with the various candidates before deciding which group she favors."

Laughing gaily, Ellena offered more information. "Our dear daughter is not like most, as I am sure you all have discovered by now. She already has your measure, having traveled with her fathers to announce her coming of age. And unlike many brides, who give an easy win to the triad of their choice by coming up with some ridiculously simple challenge, Jemina has decided to put you all to the test. For your first challenge, your triads will face off with my little warrior. She will await your groups in the center of the training field. Your task is to relieve Jemina of her sword."

Tyler spoke up as the others tried to process the information. "Relieve her of her sword in what manner?"

"Your triad will have to determine as such," she explained with a wide smile. "It won't be easy. The challenge will take place today, but the timing will remain a mystery. Until then, you may discuss the challenge among yourselves and make plans. When my youngest, Finnigan, takes up his horn, simply follow the sound. It will lead you to Jemina and your first challenge. May the Creator inspire you well."

8

Jemina's Challenge

"You are meant to move counterclockwise for this portion of the ceremony," Aras instructed Loinbard when the younger man began moving into the leader's path. Correcting his direction was an easy fix.

Glancing toward Anders, he pointed out another flaw they needed to correct. "We agreed you could keep the part of your pledge invoking the name of Finn rather than Konrad, but don't forget to recite the rest of the oath using the same words my brother and I do, or it will not have the full hypnotic effect."

"Is it so important for our chant to be in unison? After cycles of practicing with my first triad, it is hard to switch to something new." Anders kept moving and the three men worked on measuring their footwork as the circle they covered slowly closed inward.

Aras used his raised hand to help them keep count of the moves they made left before switching to the right. "You have made remarkable progress in the short time we have begun practicing together. Do not lose hope. It is true Jemina is not a city bride we need to lull into cooperation before staking our claim. Yet, if she is indeed planning to challenge her suitors to disarm her in battle, it is best to keep her calm and a bit off balanced when we disarm her. One mistake, and she might accidentally harm herself with the weapon."

Loinbard found himself starting to feel the natural rhythm of the ritual dance they followed. The chant was easy for him to master since he had heard other fledglings labor to memorize the words. "Hurt herself?" he said when they broke for a brief rest. "Have you forgotten what her father said? She is a skilled warrior, or do you disbelieve him?"

Accepting a cup of water from Anders, Aras pointed to a clear patch of grass where they could recline. "We will survive any nicks or bruises she manages to inflict. Our little gem is too honorable to wound anyone not posing an imminent threat to her or someone she loves." Downing the contents of his cup, he leaned back and observed the clouds gently move across the morning sky. "Skilled at battle or not, she is as untamed as the mist above. She needs a firm, guiding wind to help chart her courses, protecting her from raining down her fury until the time is right."

"You asked earlier about my thoughts on scolding a wife," Anders studied the clouds as well. "Were she our wife, and if she truly means to face off with three triads of trained warriors to prove her worth, I would upend her the moment I managed to remove the sword from her hand. Hendrix and Johan have no integrity. If they thought it would improve their position, they would inflict a great deal of harm to her before her fathers or anyone else could intervene."

"As leader of our group, I claim first right to administer such a correction. You may take over the task after I have reddened her ass," Aras concluded. Noon was quickly approaching and he got to his feet. "You may cover the tops of her thighs if you choose."

"And what am I to do?" Loinbard demanded, pushing his brother hard as they walked to their positions before practicing their courtship dance once again. He had been trying to trip his sibling, but didn't even manage to earn a flinch.

"We will leave the lecturing to you," Anders chuckled. "Do either of you believe we have a chance of winning this challenge using this plan? Your fellow Konrads are off practicing their disarming skills. Sage has managed to make Tyler and Riley drop their sword several times." He jerked his head toward where the men in question stood.

"Sage drew blood each time he wedged his weapon at his opponents' hand. If Jem's fathers do not take exception to him injuring their daughter, I certainly will." Aras' face was dark. He had been trained to protect his fellow Konrads, but the thought of anyone harming the woman he loved enraged him. Abruptly stopping, he found himself colliding with his blood brother. Loinbard shoved him back for the insult, this time managing to send him falling on his ass. Loved? Aras was dazed a moment. Was it possible? He, a man who swore never to give his heart to someone who would die and leave him alone, in love?

Anders offered him a hand as Aras moved to gain his feet. "Are you ill?" the Finn warrior asked. The blaring of Finnegan's horn saved Aras from answering. Snatching up their belongings, they followed the sound toward the first challenge.

THE MANNER in which the competing triads studied the training fields surprised Jemina at first. Realization slowly dawned. Villages must have unique set ups for their training fields and family units. Her eyes looked up at the nine men on the top level. The layout of the drilling ground had been designed to mimic the family unit structures of Urijah. The ground level was widest. In homes, this is the area the family warriors protected. The section was marked off in thirds, marking the area each person in the triad was responsible for keeping secure.

If breached, attackers would have access to the next level below the ground. Here less skilled members of a family unit were stationed, their sole goal to stop any outsiders from reaching the lowest, third level, where sucklings and wives were found.

No floor and secret door hid one level from the next on the training field. Part of the learning process involved each member of a fighting team to witness the destruction caused by his failure to protect those below.

Teams of fledglings were clustered together by leaders and formed strong bonds, learning to honestly assess each member's strengths and voting each person's placement on the levels according to this knowledge. A skilled student on the top section had to watch and explain to his trainers the ramifications of allowing an enemy past their section, narrating each mock murder and advancement of challenging groups.

Jemina, herself, heard echoes from past training sessions that still haunted her cycles later. For a moment, she was a child of seventeen again. It was her first time serving on the top level. She had worked hard to make her way up from the bottom, taking pride when her training partners deemed her worthy to cover ground level. But the pressure was unyielding there, something she had never considered. Every slight miscalculation she made had far reaching ramifications for others. No one was really hurt in these trials, but the certainty of what reality could bring due to failure was gut wrenching.

"How many members of your 'family unit' died in this fight, fledgling?" A harsh trainer yelled beside her, rain pouring down from the sky, masking the tears falling from her eyes as she watched those below her level. "Twelve, sir."

He spouted off a memorized lecture every fledgling had to suffer through. She had heard him give it to others, but never taken it to heart before. "Do you see the small child lying in that muddy puddle on the bottom floor? He could be your son, the baby your wife, er, the baby you just blessed your family unit with. His fate is bleak if your performance today is any indication of how you would handle a threat on his life. Do you feel you are ready to leave these training fields and act as a warrior for the Village of Urijah?"

"No sir. I ask permission to go down a level at the next trial." Pride had not made her blind. "I still have much to learn as a fledgling, sir."

Other trials had followed, her performance improving exponentially She had made her way back to the ground level again, and officially graduated a month before being labeled of age and ready to marry. Jemina had been determined not to marry until she was secure in the knowledge she could protect those who depended on her. But that first experience on the top level still haunted her.

"Papa Ellias, make her explain the challenge so I can stop blowing this blasted horn. I am all out of air." Finnegan's complaint brought her back to the present. Eyes focused on her opponents again, she blocked out all but the task at hand.

"The first challenge is easy enough to understand. On my word, the event will commence. To win, your triad has to be the first to remove my sword from my hand."

"Is each triad meant to take turns approaching you?" Anders sought clarification. He looked displeased with the entire task. While she still considered him, Aras and Loinbard her true mates and was sure the Creator would ensure they won her hand, she felt the triad needed to gain some respect for her. This was one sure way to make it happen.

"You may sit and await the other triads' attempts, if you choose, sir, but I will impose no limits on who advances toward me. May the Creator be on your side. Begin." She lifted her weapon in a mock salute and lifted her chin as if daring anyone to approach.

The Konrad triad and Aras' group took time to consider how to proceed. The warriors from Finn, namely Hendrix and Johan, wasted no time. Ignoring Crosby, they leapt down the middle level before separating. They meant to strike at her from opposite ends, advancing on her so she did not have time to plan her reaction.

Jemina spotted Aras' look of alarm from the top level. He ordered her to watch her back, but she did not even acknowledge the command. She remained frozen in her spot, like an owl blinded by a torch carried along a dark night. Hendrix's smile was insulting as he moved closer and closer, his eyes locked on her sword. He stopped only an arm's length away and waited as his brother crept up on her from behind. "I cannot wait until I have you in my bed, innocent Jemina. You have no idea of the wicked pleasures you will learn to bestow on me."

Johan snuck closer, his fist reaching out to yank the sword from her hand. A bellow of outrage filled the area as she twisted at the last moment, moving her weapon up and across, slashing a thin line across the man's bronzed forearm. Her attention was back on Hendrix before either man could process her attack.

"In my village, husbands are charged with bestowing pleasures on their wife. We might not be suited, sir. There is still time to remove yourself from the competition." Jemina lunged toward him without warning, marking his mocking face with a cut across the right cheek.

For several moments, she moved in ways neither man could predict, slicing shallow nicks over their forearms, necks and hands. They had left their weapons on the top level, arrogant enough to assume they would not need them to challenge a mere woman. Now enraged, they turned to climb back up and retrieve them.

Jemina feared she might have to do serious damage if they decided to return armed to fight. She watched them circle the top-level, looking for where they left their swords. Loinbard, who had the most engaging smile, pointed toward an observation deck where her parents were watching. Someone had tossed the Finn swords to her fathers, and they were now out of reach.

Hendrix, red with frustration, started to charge toward his weapon, Johan at his heels. Only after the two men were well off the grass covering the first level of the training field did Jemina call out a warning. "Did I forget to mention the part about any man leaving the area being disqualified? How unfortunate. Better luck with the next task, men of Finn."

The Konrad triad decided to try their luck. Tyler and Riley were tasked with occupying Aras, Loinbard and Anders on the top level while Sage moved lower to try his hand at disarming Jemina. He had his sword, but was using great care not to wield it in a manner that might bring harm to her. She found the consideration endearing and sincerely regretted the nasty cut she inflicted on his weapon hand. She used the tip of her sword to guide the Konrad weapon out of reach. She did not wish to hurt him, but if he kept swinging the blade in her direction, she would have no choice.

"You might want to see our healer, Dalia for some healing herbs to make sure that cut doesn't get infected."

Crosby was lingering by the edge of the top level, looking confused by the events unfolding. Jemina heard Johan demand the attractive warrior go after her sword. She really wished Crosby would not listen. Using her blade on him would be like attacking a clueless child. Sage was wrapping his bleeding wrist and climbing up the levels when Crosby moved down.

He wore white, Jemina grimaced. What warrior came to battle in white? Instead of covering his shirt with blood, she flicked the tip of her sword left and right, slashing rips across the material. It was hard not to be proud of herself. Not a hint of blood marred the shirt. Crosby did not realize how lucky he had been and complained as he left the area.

Tyler and Riley cautiously approached, leaving their weapons behind. "I don't suppose you would hand over your weapon willingly?" Riley asked with a boyish smile.

"Would you?" She grinned, slightly nicking both men's skin as they tried to sneak close enough to yank the weapon away. Not willing to risk harming the village bride they sought to claim, Jemina watched the Konrad warriors collect their things and leave the field.

Only Aras, Loinbard and Anders remained on the training field with her now. If she were smart, her mother had told her before they came to the field, she would toss the sword at this triad's feet and be joyful they were ahead in the competition. Jemina knew she was smart, but was not above allowing her stubborn pride to muddle her thoughts. She wanted to prove herself to these men before they laid claim to her. Respect should be established before mating, to her way of thinking.

The three men slowly moved about the top level, positioning themselves an equal distance apart, and she felt disappointment. Instead of giving her praise for defeating their challengers, these men were obviously going to try and outwit her, too. So much for gaining their respect. She lifted her sword and prepared for battle.

But instead of starting down the levels, the three men began circling the top. They moved as one, first left, then right, fast than slow, and as they moved, they chanted in low tones. Lowering her weapon, she strained to hear their words. If they moved to attack, she would have plenty of time to react, for they were so far away. "Chosen bride, we claim you as ours."

Shaking her head, she decided she was not hearing correctly. The men seemed to be closing in their circle as they danced around the top level, the whispers drifting in bits and pieces to her section below. "Protect you… honor you… gift you with our seed…" The measure of their movement was hypnotizing, making her heart beat slow down, her muscles relax. "The Village of Konrad is pleased to welcome you, bride."

The men had somehow made their way down to the second level, but she was too confused by the contrasting chants of the Konrad warriors from the Finn fighter. He clearly named his own village, and added his people would be honored for her to bear their lineage in her womb. Then the chant became one again, the movement matching the beat of their steps now. "Chosen bride, we claim you as ours to protect. We will honor you above all others. Please accept the gift of our seed and bless us with many children."

Were they performing the mating dance? Jemina was stunned. Such traditions did not take place until a bride was to be claimed. Her brother and his triad, along with all others in the village, had to master the complex movements and pledge to be given when they wed. It took cycles to grasp the skill. Hadn't this triad just formed? And why would they make their pledge now, before they had even been declared winners of the competition?

Their dance brought them down into her area now. She did not lift her sword high, but kept it poised to bring up when the time came. She would do her best to only scar small portions of each man. She did not wish to face the rest of her life with men who resented her for besting them in battle.

Anders was directly in front of her now, preparing to twist about for the next part of the dance. Jemina kept Loinbard and Aras' placement in mind, knowing a surprise attack was more likely to come than a frontal maneuver. It was Anders' misstep that broke her concentration. He stumbled, and his large frame hit the ground with a mighty thud. Her father Leodon yelled out an alert, but she did not hear it in time to stop what followed.

Aras was at her side without warning, gently claiming her lips, his hands raised high to prove he was not a threat. The rightness of their mouths touching made Jemina sigh, and she stepped closer to him. His hard hands slowly lowered to her face, and he tilted her head so he could thrust his tongue between her lips. The sensations pouring across her body confused her.

The sword in her hand was eased away, but she did not protest. Instead she lifted her hands to Aras' waist, trying to find her balance as the world seemed to spin around her. When he pulled away from her, Jemina lifted her hand to touch her swollen lips in awe.

A sound smack applied to her backside had her twirling around, reeling about to face an attacker. She found Aras shaking his finger at her. "That was for putting yourself in danger. Do it again, and I will bare your arse before we each take turns instructing you on the importance of your safety."

"How dare you strike a village daughter!" Jemina yelped, wishing she had come up with something better to say.

The second smack was more unexpected than the first. Anders, no longer laying on the ground in apparent pain, was by her side. "I will kill any man who dares to raise a sword at you, even if it is only to relieve you of your weapon. If I learn you challenged him to do so, you will not sit comfortably for many days and nights."

Then the devil bent down to kiss her. Before she could object, he turned to start climbing back up the different levels. Jemina was quite upset with herself for not expecting the third hard hand that assaulted her backside. She was ready to jab Loinbard with her sword when she recalled she had somehow lost it.

His lips pressed hard against hers, his tongue boldly darting inside. Loinbard backed away with a grin before offering the weapon back to her. Jemina realized the entire process that got them to this point had been orchestrated by the triad so they could win the challenge. Anders fall, Aras' kiss, Loinbard ending up with her sword.

She had wanted to earn their respect, but ended up gaining a bit of it herself. A smile touched her lips. She promised herself she would still find a way to repay their rude scolding and physical attack on her person. But first, she wanted to enjoy more of their kissing.

9

Lasting Promise

Ellias stood ready to face off with the triad from Konrad and Finn. The liberties the men had taken during Jemina's challenge enraged him. The tense manner Darnish and Leodon held themselves confirmed they were furious, too. Had any of them carried their sword to this arena, they certainly would have pulled it now as they waited. "Sons of Konrad and Finn," Ellias roared, "in front of all present, I wish to tell you…"

"The first win goes to your triad," Ellena finished for him, earning a nasty glare from her husbands. She faced them with a polite smile. "The challenge was set and the rules announced. By our daughter's own words. To win, a triad had to be the first to remove the sword from her hand."

"No warrior has been successful in unarming Jemina for two cycles, wife. It was the only reason we allowed such a ridiculous event in the first place." Leodon took a step toward Aras. Both Jemina and her mother stepped forward to block his path.

Darnish glared at them. "You both were convinced none of the triads would be able to claim a victory today."

"This was purely a lesson so her suitors would gain respect for her before the real competition commenced," Ellias pointed out. "Yet now you seek to assign a winner. Tis the truth wife, I would toss two of the triads out now, had we not already agreed to let them take part." Rounding on the triad from Finn, he addressed Hendrix personally. "I may be older than you, but my hearing is excellent. Dare you speak to my daughter in such a vulgar way again, and I will ensure the paltry wounds she inflicted will be multiplied by ten."

Johan was quick to defend his brother. "He employed shocking words to gain an advantage against a fighter threatening him with a sword. Neither he or I physically struck your daughter or laid our lips upon hers. That insult came from the Konrad triad alone."

"You acted like childish warriors, daring to come in search for your weapons when your pride was stung by a superior fighter." Ellena flashed a deadly expression at Johan until he backed away. Then she addressed her mates again. "Tis the truth, Jemina and I had no way of knowing Aras, Anders and Loinbard would approach the challenge in such an unusual manner, but it would be dishonorable to deny them a win which they clearly earned."

Ellias motioned for his triad to join him. They spent a few moments conferring before coming to an agreement. "Our wife speaks the truth. The Village of Urijah will not go back on the rules announced. Know this. We will take great care to think carefully about what determines the victories in future challenges. Ellena and Jemina, you will escort our wounded guests to the healer's compound."

Both women seemed displeased with the suggestion and exchanged a secret look. Ellena smiled sweetly and started to suggest their daughter show the men while she stayed behind. Leodon cut her off.

"We will join you there after we have a private meeting with the winning triad. This is not open to debate. You can explain any displeasure with this choice later, in the privacy of our family unit. We will be ready to share our own disappointment in today's proceedings then, too."

Jemina sought to object, but her mother quickly grabbed her hand and led her away. "Follow us, Sage, Riley, Tyler, and you lot," she called to the injured warriors.

Once alone, the fathers started circling Aras, Loinbard and Anders, their wrath apparent. "How dare any of you lay claim to our daughter's lips," Ellias condemned.

"Much less assume the right to discipline her," Darnish censured.

"Those rights belong to the triad which weds her." Leodon spat. "The wedding dance and pledging chant are not things to be mocked and manipulated so you can win a contest. With this win, you have lost our respect, men of Konrad and Finn. Think you for a moment we will soon forget this insult and award you anymore wins?"

"We were not mocking the dance or pledge," Anders held his head high.

"Both were performed as should be, when a triad has determined a bride they lay claim to, sir," Loinbard clarified.

"You have not been awarded our daughter's hand in marriage," Ellias yelled, his temper palpable now. "Jemina has not given her pledge to you."

"Without winning the competition," Darnish pointed out, "you just promised to give your love, protection and seed to one woman. Another triad may win. Are your vows so meaningless you will offer them again to a second bride?"

"Win her hand or not," Aras said, his eyes locked on Ellias', "the pledge was given in good faith. Our triad has claimed Jemina as our wife. Even if she marries another, we will never do so. The dance and chant were official declarations for all to see. Our triad will claim no other woman, even if it means we never are able to form an official family unit. We all agreed to this before deciding to perform the dance and chant."

"Do you understand exactly what you three are asserting?" Leodon asked and each of the younger warriors nodded the affirmation without hesitation. The three fathers' postures became less threatening at this news. "I wish you luck then, triad of Konrad and Finn."

"Though we cannot favor you in future challenges," Darnish said, extending his hand to Aras, "know you have reclaimed our respect. Now let's join the others at the healer's compound before our wife and daughter sneak back to make sure we haven't slaughtered you all."

Loinbard laughed at the words, sure the older man was jesting. The serious expression on each father's face had him swallowing the sound. "The compound is this way, right?"

ARAS PULLED his sword free and cautiously advanced. A few feet ahead, his lovely Jemina stood unaware a vicious hound was directly behind her. The animal sensed their approach and bared his fangs in the warriors' direction. He had fought creatures like this before, while roaming between the second set of walls at the city, of all places. This one claimed more sharp teeth than those beasts. He also had an extra, sharp toe claw on both front paws.

Sword raised high, Aras knew he must kill the animal before it could do harm to Jemina. The beast was not the only one who was aware of his arrival. Jemina turned to give him a welcoming smile before noticing his intent. "Aras, don't you dare harm my pet!" she ordered, grabbing the fierce animal by the scruff and pulling him behind her. The animal whimpered like a pup.

She patted his head gently, giving him words of praise. "You did well, warning me about an approaching threat. I am proud of you, Smiley. What a good boy you are." She started scratching underneath the beast's chin, bending down to hug him around the neck next. Stowing his weapon, Aras wished he was as lucky as the dog.

Anders and Loinbard reached where he stood. They had been farther back, walking in step with the fathers, unaware of Aras' concern. Now they noticed the way the woman they claimed as bride glared at him. "That is not the expression of a happy woman," his brother teased him.

"Try not to blow our advantage in the competition. We want to win her approval, not her fury," Anders said his words slowly, as if trying to advise a small child who was struggling to discern the complex rules of a game.

"The hound at her feet is her pet," Aras announced. "She calls it Smiley."

Loinbard made his way forward, slowly extending his hand so the animal could sniff it. The dog was cautious at first, but when Jemina gave an approving nod, it licked his palm. "You look like a Smiley with all those extra teeth. I've encountered hounds like this outside my village during my hunts. They generally avoid humans. How did you manage to befriend it, much less let the guards surrounding your village allow it within the borders?"

"Our healer raises dogs," Jemina explained, favoring him with a smile before cutting a disappointing look toward Aras. "The warriors assumed Smiley was one of her animals. I found him as a pup just outside the village boundary. The poor thing was skin and bones. I nursed him back to health and he has been my pet ever since."

"My apologies for planning to harm your pet." Hoping to make up for the offense, Aras came forward and tried to pat the animal's head. It growled and flashed its abundance of teeth at him. Thanks to his years of training as a warrior, Aras did not back away, but it was difficult. He hoped changing the subject might improve Jemina's temperament. "How are the other triads?"

"Dalia has patched them up," she told him. "Come, I will show you inside her compound so you can see for yourself." Aras did step back them. His distrust of healers was impossible to hide. "There is nothing to be worried about," Jemina told him. "There is nothing inside but healing herbs and such. Don't you have a healer in your village?"

Loinbard did not trust healers either, but he was able to contain his feelings. "We have a healer, but she does not raise hounds."

Nodding as if she understood now, Jemina tried to sooth Aras' concerns. "Her animals are well mannered. She breeds them carefully to bring out useful traits, but none are used for fighting, if that is what causes your apprehension."

"I would like to see inside the healer's first circle," Anders announced, unaware of his new brothers' strange suspicion of healers. "How did Hendrix and Johan handle having to seek medical attention after their defeat. It is not honorable for me to find pleasure in their humiliation," he said. "Yet I do, so you must tell me everything you noticed. Feel free to exaggerate their pain."

"You are not still dealing with the frustration of them tossing you out of their triad?" Jemina teased. "Don't you find your new group more suitable?"

"As much as it pains me to admit as much, Hendrix and Johan gave me the best gift of all my life. By rejecting me, they freed me to form a much better, honorable alliance with Aras and Loinbard. Still, it would please me to know they have suffered from their hasty decision."

Laughing with understanding, Jemina put her arm through his, and ushered Anders inside. "Hendrix asked for something to dull the pain before allowing Dalia to stitch up the wound on his face. Johan was too proud to do so, and the sting brought tears to his eyes. He put it off as a reaction to the hound hair in the compound, but no one else was fooled."

Aras and Loinbard followed, uncomfortable with entering the healer's domain, but unwilling to let Jemina out of their sight so long as Hendrix or Johan were nearby. "Why didn't you cut Crosby as you did the others?" Aras asked.

"It would be a shame to mar his beauty," she told him. Jealousy filled his mind with images of disfiguring Crosby so Jemina would not wish to gaze upon him. She was turned away from him and did not notice. "Appearance is the sole strength the poor man has," she told Anders. "Why would any triad ever think trading you for him would give them an advantage?"

Loinbard was happy to explain. "According to them, you fell madly in love with Crosby after laying eyes on his perfect features."

"I did not notice his features first," Jemina said. She looked at Anders again as she continued, "I saw his hair and mistook it for yours."

Aras noticed how her eyes grew wide. What had her strange words meant? Before he could question her, she threw open the door to the first circle in the village's healing building. "Do not worry about the hounds you see inside. They are well behaved. And don't try to kill any of them," she told Aras with a weary look. "Dalia won't forgive such a mistake, and you are likely to require her healing skills at some point in your time here."

He did not hesitate to reply. "I am pleased you are concerned about my welfare, village bride, but you need not worry. My brother or Anders will stitch up any wounds I may gain. I do not put my faith in healers. In my experience, they have hidden agendas."

The first level of the healer's building reeked of subterfuge. Aras began studying the floor in search of the hidden entrance to the level just below. Then the large cases lining the wall caught his attention. The rest of his triad and Jemina's fathers sought the spot where the wounded men were resting. Aras headed toward the strange shelves full of jars that lined the walls. There had to be hundreds of the tiny containers, and each had a label filled with detailed notes.

Lifting one, he found it cold to the touch as if it was being protected by some type of coolant to preserve the contents inside. He silently read the label. "Sperm of alpha male, gray pack. Offspring bred should be skilled in tracking through smell."

"You must be highly regarded in your village," Jemina told him as he replaced the jar. She followed along as he scanned the different labels. "Few here read. Unless the elders deem it important, most males train solely for defending. Yet you are clever at both reading and defending. Are you slated to be a village elder one day?"

"My second mother insisted everyone in our family unit learn how to read. Knowledge is power she insisted. Secret text might provide needed information to preparing oneself for future battles."

"You are a very solemn man, Aras." She moved closer, and he could smell her beautiful hair. It reminded him of exotic fruit, rare and addictive. "I can see determination in your face. What past battles haunt you?"

Aras reached up to trace the soft curve down her chin. His thumb touched her bottom lip, pulling it down playfully, exposing the inside. "When you are my wife, there will be no secrets between us, my precious Jem. Any battles I wage will be your fight as well. Until then, I must remain silent."

"At first, I thought the one called Crosby was your favorite, Jemina." A husky voice startled them from their intimate moment, and Aras turned to find a frizzy-hair woman approaching. "He is the only man of the original competitors unmarked by your sword. Then this last triad came in, and I realized they might hold your heart. None of them need my service. You appear to favor this particular one more than the others." The healer was frowning toward Aras as she spoke again. "Your fathers might object to his holding your hand."

Until the strange woman mentioned it, Aras had not even realized he was clutching Jemina's smaller fingers in his own. Reluctantly he prepared to let it go, but she gripped it tightly. "Dalia, meet Aras, from the village of Konrad. I shared your hobby in breeding hounds with him. He was studying your collection of seed."

"I noticed. This entire section is devoted to animals genetically bred to be superior trackers. Think of how much easier the life of a warrior could be if dogs carried their supplies, or better yet, pulled provisions and man behind some type of sleigh."

"The village elders of Urijah sanction your placing yourself in the role of Creator?" He made no effort to hide his abhorrence of this woman's role. She, like Ulthia, the healer of his own village, had a hidden role as thieves. Jemina sought to soften his rudeness, but he squeezed her hand as a silent warning not to get involved.

"What family unit in Konrad do you come from?" Delia's eyes narrowed.

"One you have no doubt feared for many cycles now, healer." Aras held himself tall as he continued, "Remind your friends of the promise made. It is the only thing stopping us from exposing the city's secrets."

Unable to contain herself, Jemina spoke, "Dalia is not from the city. Not anymore. She's been here many generations now. She harbors no city secret. Trust me, she could not speak to the women of the city, even if she chose to, because no woman is allowed outside of our border."

"I recall one woman traveling freely past your village limits," Aras replied. "Though I am sure you sought the permission of your elders to do so. There are ways around such restrictions." Removing the jar of hound sperm in his hand, Dalia set it back in place before walking away.

"You have insulted her," Jemina fretted and he pulled her close to console her.

"Where is Smiley's seed stored on this wall?" he whispered his question.

"Dalia breeds her animals for specific traits. My pet's imperfections need to be weaned out of future generations according to the healer," she explained.

Aras could see her confusion. She did not understand how any of this involved the insulting, mysterious words he had just shared with the healer. She already knew too much, and this was not the time, nor place to discuss such sensitive matters. It was wrong to burden Jemina with his knowledge of the city's secrets. One day, when they were wed, she would need to understand the whole situation. But not now.

"It pleases me to know you accept the Creator's hounds as they are, extra teeth and all."

"His looks mean nothing," Jemina argued. "Look at Crosby. He is easy to look upon, but the most important traits are lacking. His loyalty is questionable if the changing of triads is any indication. As for skill, my loyal pet could track me down and would give his life to protect me if needed. Crosby lacks the necessary skills to protect himself, much less others."

He could not resist giving her a brief kiss. "You are wise beyond measure. Understand this, dear village bride, some judge creatures by qualities they consider more worthy, inadvertently eliminating things like loyalty or less noticeable qualities. To do so is shortsighted and often leads to unpredictable flaws in future generations. The results cost innocent people their very lives."

"Explain further," she demanded.

"In time, my rare Jem."

10

Gaining a Sister

"'Tis the truth, I wish we had more time to get to know each other, Giannis. There is much I still do not know about you." Jemina walked alongside her new sister-in-law before the evening meal.

The younger girl gave a delightful laugh, her fawn colored hair framing her enchanting face. "Having you around longer to help me adjust to the village would be wonderful. Things here are so foreign from what is normal in the city."

"What's it like?" Jemina often speculated about things in the city, a place of all women who did not have to seek permission from men to follow their dreams.

"Stifling," the other woman responded, surprising the village bride. "Everything is so predictable there. Each woman has a duty to perform. Be you a virgin born or a Godsend, nothing separates you from those around you. No one is special or unique. Only the elders get a bit of power or control over their existence, but even they prefer not to stand out. We are taught often from an early age that being an individual is selfish. Everyone must instead strive to improve the community and fade into the crowd."

"Virgin born?" Jemina stopped walking and sought clarification. "Godsend?"

"The Creator sends newborn babies to the city. They are labeled as Godsends. These babies just appear within the breeding building at the very center of our city without announcement, sometimes as many as four baby girls show up in any given cycle."

Jemina pointed to a large rock beneath an oak tree where they could sit and continue their discussion. "May I braid your hair for you?" she asked. When Giannis nodded, she started portioning off the thick strands and working her fingers through the silky mane to brush out a few knots. "Please tell me more about the Godsends."

Not used to being pampered, Giannis happily closed her eyes while enjoying the treatment. "I have heard others talk about there being three different openings in the breeding area's lowest level. It is considered holy land and only priestesses are allowed below. This is where angels deposit the babies."

Completely relaxed, the city bride continued sharing details of where she once lived. "Where each child appears determines which priestess is in charge of the baby girl's future. That's what our leaders are called: priestesses, not elders. They keep very thorough birth records, mentioning which opening a babe appeared at, the cycle and moon's placement in the heavens. In addition, they are in charge of deciding which nursery the girls should grow up in, and the types of jobs they will be allowed to pursue as they get older."

People mingled around them as children and women went about preparing the dining area for the evening meal. No one paid much attention to Jemina or Giannis, unless one counted Jael and Loinbard. It was customary for brides not to be left out of sight of at least one of their new husbands. Giannis' youngest husband protected her now. Jemina did not realize that Loinbard was doing the same where she was concerned. The warrior from

Konrad listened attentively, taking in every bit of information he could glean about city life to share with Aras later.

Jemina had a horrible thought and considered not speaking it. But Giannis was her new friend and sister. They should be able to share secrets or suspicions without fear. "In our village, others too, if what I have heard is to be trusted, babies sometimes go missing from our healer's compound. You don't suppose... Could it be possible someone is stealing our babies and bringing them to the city?"

Turning to face her, Giannis shared her thoughts. "I used to wonder at the miracle of Godsends often, especially since the building where they appear is near the center of the city. I find it even more astounding now that I know three walls separate any outsiders from being able to sneak a newborn within. I have only been on two of the three levels in Dalia's compound, but they look impenetrable, too." She blushed, not being able to bring herself to mention being claimed by her husbands there, as was tradition in the villages. "How could someone steal a baby from within?"

"Warriors guard our walls and fathers protect the birthing area of the compound. There is no logical way I can think how a mortal could steal a baby from a village," Jemina said, but her mind still pondered the matter.

Giannis nodded her understanding. "Clearly the Creator alone has such skills, though why there is even such a need, I cannot understand, because of the city's mastery of virgin birth. It is a bit complicated, and I am not smart enough to understand, much less explain, the process. Most of the city's citizens come from this method of birth. The scientists in our medical unit have perfected using the egg of one woman and the DNA of another to breed babies. This helps keep the number of citizens within the city at a healthy rate."

With a guilty smile, Giannis bent closer to her new friend to share a secret. "After the first two claimings, I must admit it seems foolish to deny the pleasure a man can afford a breeder."

The evening meal would commence soon or Jemina might have considered asking for more details on the subject of mating. Now that her dream lovers had proven to be flesh and blood men, she longed to know if any of her sexy dreams were mere fantasy, or even physically possible. "What happens to the male children who come from this virgin born process?" Jemina was still fascinated with city life. Aras' comments about humans trying to become creators mingling with Giannis' description of virgin births.

"The process only results in female children. Even the Godsends are always feminine. I guess such is the Creator's wisdom, because males are not accepted within the city limits. I can only assume any male children would be left outside the city walls."

"Surely to do that would be the same as murdering the babe. How could anyone turn their back on an innocent child, male or female?" The village bride thanked the Creator for allowing her to be born outside the city. Her twin brother would be disposed of like an unwanted pet had their mother given birth in the city.

"The priestesses in our city are adamant that all males grow into hostile creatures cursed to kill or maim those around them," Giannis elucidated.

"If they left an innocent babe outside their walls, they would be guilty of murder, and no better than the men they reject." Jemina was filled with outrage. She, from her very conception, had been surrounded by males. Within her mother's womb, she grew alongside Jael. Since birth, she had tagged along after him, learning the skills and respecting how being male and female gave each their own set of skills and strengths.

ARAS FOLLOWED Smiley as he moved around the various tables where people took their meal. The hound moved about, weaving in and out of paths, until he located whom he searched for in the large crowd. "Do diners change where they sit each meal?" he asked, taking a seat across from Jemina.

"Not generally, but there are some exceptions. Last night and this morning," she buttered a piece of bread and passed it to him, "we ate at the bridal table. Giannis and her husbands are still there now, but Chaim and Moshe have extended family members. Many of them could not fit, so our family unit offered to return to our usual table to allow them to move there. "How did you ever find us in this crowd? I was just about to send my fathers in search of you when you arrived."

"Your pet led me here. Does he often sit close by, hoping for scraps of food?"

She leaned down to see Smiley hiding out of sight under the table. Shaking her head at him, she tried to warn Aras not to give the animal's presence away. "He's not allowed in this area, especially if food is being consumed. He must have escaped his pen near our family unit."

Aras smiled and gave her a wink. Leaning closer, he said, "Your secret is safe with me, my Jem. How did he find this table, I wonder?"

Gifting him with a bright smile, she leaned forward herself. "He can track me no matter where I am in the village. The only reason he did not come with my fathers and me when we left to announce the wedding competition was because Dalia kept him tied up with her own hounds while we were gone. She says he cried the entire time I was away."

"Being in your presence is quite addictive." He smiled before nodding a greeting to Loinbard at her right and Anders at her left. "And why are we allowed such favorable places to dine tonight? Hendrix and Johan do not seem happy that we are so close to you for this meal."

"Winner of each challenge gains prime spots at the dinner table. Had you been here earlier, you might have managed to sit at our beautiful Jemina's side," Loinbard gloated.

"I was on time for the meal," Aras pointed out, "but I went to the original table where we ate our other meals. How did you know to come here, brother?"

"As luck would have it, I was close by Jemina when the evening meal bell rang. She told me. Anders was passing by and I shared my knowledge with him." Loinbard raised an eyebrow in challenge.

"Rather than saving a chair for your own brother, you allowed another to benefit?" Aras chided in mock censure.

"Anders is my brother, too, now that we are part of the same triad. Besides, he is left-handed and you are right. He and I can sit close to Jemina without bumping into her the entire meal."

Aras observed as Jemina spent the first part of the meal listening to Loinbard as he explained an old earth game called chess. Wolf, one of their fathers, was a master of the game, and he used it to help his sons learn about various strategies. It was important to always be two steps ahead of one's opponent in the game. Jemina's eyes grew wider as Loinbard detailed the process of playing.

She smiled up at him and Aras savored observing her perfect, full lips. He watched her closely as she spoke, noticing every flick of her tongue and wishing he could tease it with his own. "So in battle, it would be wise to try to predict what your enemy plans to do so you can determine the best way to counter it? Sword fighting is much the same way. I have found many warriors concentrate on thrusting or overpowering their opponents. It's best to block and wait for an opening instead of trying to force one."

"May I sneak your pet a bit of beef?" Anders asked in a low voice and received a grin in reward. "Smiley is devoted to you. How long have you had him as a pet?"

"For three cycles now," Jemina explained. "When my twin brother Jael left to guard the wall, having Smiley at my side was the only thing which made life bearable. I mean to take him with me when I move to my husbands' village. Do you think the village elders there will balk at having him around? I don't recall seeing any other hounds running around other places."

"In the village of Finn, arrangements would need to be discussed with the elders. I assume things would be the same in Konrad. It will be interesting to see what life holds for us if we earn the gift of claiming you as a wife, Jemina. It will no doubt be humorous to see Aras and Loinbard explain not only bringing a triad member from outside the Konrad line back home, but a furious looking animal with plentiful, sharp teeth."

"Smiley is really quite harmless," Jemina promised. "Unless someone were to try and harm me. He would probably roll over and allow anyone to rub his tummy otherwise."

"Your pet seeks to protect you?" Aras asked. "I am beginning to see the wisdom of having him around. If danger is at hand and you are unable to protect yourself, it would be comforting to know Smiley is there."

"Would you allow him to sleep inside your family unit, then?" Jemina said and graced him with her own smile.

"If he was trained properly and bathed," Aras teased back.

She bent forward again, her small, pert breasts peeking out over the top of her shirt. Her expression was hopeful. "Could he share our bed if we were wed?"

"Sharing you with Loinbard and Anders would be difficult enough," he said, hating to deny her anything when Jemina looked so pleased. "You did say Smiley was protective of you. He might misunderstand your moans of pleasure for distress when your husbands seek to mate with you. I would hate for him to bite down on me, especially if I am in your arms, sharing your bed."

11

Leodon's Challenge

Konrad-Finn Triad: 1 win

"I have an uneasy feeling we are being shown the exit of the village," Anders uttered just loud enough for his triad alone to hear. "This is the way toward the outer boundaries of the village. Which one of you insulted the fathers this morning?"

"He freed the hound again this morning," Loinbard indicated toward his blood brother. "I watched him feed the beast some bits of pig meat before ordering him to lead the way to Jemina. The fathers no doubt found having a hound at the table to be insulting."

Aras shoved Loinbard. "They probably took exception to the way you gawked at Jemina from the moment she joined us for the morning meal. You acted as if you had never seen a beautiful woman before."

"I was not gawking at her so much as studying her dress," the younger Konrad warrior defended.

"Pardon me," Anders muttered in frustration, "but gawking at her body would likely be more offensive to the fathers than just staring at her lovely face."

Squeezed in between the two other members of his group, Loinbard was frustrated with his treatment and sought to clue his friends in on the matter. He swiftly reached up and slugged both men in the face with a crushing blow. A smile of pride touched his lips when he heard the cartilage from Aras' nose give way. Neither of his targets could retaliate without bringing attention to themselves. Aras reached up to snap his nose back in place, clearing away some of the blood with his sleeve. A slight trickle of blood kept flowing, but it did not appear to bother him. His step did not falter the entire time.

"I was not ogling Jemina's body, though it is remarkable. Her breasts are the perfect size, just big enough to cup with a hand or suckle." Loinbard digressed. "It was the cloth of her dress which intrigued me. Our second mother, Attie had one like it."

"Attie never wore such a dress in my presence," Aras said as he slyly drove his elbow into his brother's ribs. He grinned when the younger man could not suppress a groan. Jemina's fathers suddenly stopped leading the triads toward some unknown end point. They turned around to investigate the sound. Deciding to provide some plausible explanation, Aras addressed them directly. "My brother ate a large portion of pig meat this morning. His bowels are protesting now." Aras turned to Loinbard and challenged, "Do you need us to wait a bit for you to regain control?"

"I am fine," his brother grunted, and the fathers turned back around.

Anders waited until the other triads passed them up to deliver a crashing blow to Loinbard's nose. Ever the gentlemen, the warrior from Finn reset it for Loinbard before making clear the reasoning behind his action. "In the village of Finn, we embrace the old earth adage, an eye for an eye. In this case, it would be a nose for a nose. Now explain more about the dress. I noted its quality, myself. It appeared to be a first-generation relic."

Aras froze for a moment, recalling an occasion where his

second mother had worn a ceremonial gown much like the one Jemina donned today. "You are right about the dress. The day after her second or third claiming," he told Loinbard. "Attie had one much like it on. Kia's mother was distressed by it. I assume that is why she never put it on again after that one time."

The triad continued to discuss the matter as they hung back, careful to keep their eyes on the men before them, but far enough away to allow for privacy. Loinbard continued, "We were mere boys at the time, but I remember the dress because it was the first time I had ever heard mention of a first-generation heirloom. I asked Otto to explain it's meaning to me, but he brushed my question aside. That in itself was unusual because he generally doted on us. Otto is the most respected of our village elders." He explained to Anders.

Loinbard tasted a hint of blood and realized his nose had been bleeding. He smeared the red stain across his face with a careless attempt to clean up. "Otto seemed to be quite shocked when he realized our father gave it to Attie in the first place. Speaking of the dress seemed to disturb him, and for a moment, I thought the wise, hardened warrior might shed a tear or two over mere garb. His reaction made me even more curious, and I wanted to study it carefully to see what made it so special, but Attie never wore it again. I wonder what happened to it?"

"Only a select group of villagers possess such relics or boast of the right to wear them. Could our bride be a direct descendent of Urijah?" Anders suggested. "That would be an even rarer find than a village born girl."

"The more I get to know her, the stronger my feelings for Jemina become." Aras noticed the men in front had halted and were waiting for them to join the group. The border of the village was mere feet ahead. Extra warriors lined the area now. Were they needed for added security? "Direct descendent or not, I would seek Jemina's hand no matter what. Even if she were a city born bride."

"I agree completely," Anders scanned around them, taking in every detail to prepare for whatever they might face.

Loinbard inclined his head to the right, cluing his triad on the placement of young men in the trees. "My blood brother knows I swore never to marry a city bride, but were our 'gem' from the city, I would break that oath without regret. Everything about her feels as it should be. Even our triad, born strictly to improve our chance to compete for her hand feels right. We have worked together for mere days, but our allegiance is stronger than many other triads I have known for cycles. Jemina is our one true match. Let's do everything in our power to make sure no one else steals her away from us."

Leodon gained everyone's attention before slowly articulating his words, pausing now and again to see if anyone had questions before continuing. Aras was relieved to discover the triads were not being forced to leave the village. This was where the next challenge would begin. The more solemn of Jemina's fathers had no doubt concocted this event. Every detail and potential loophole had been considered.

"Any husbands who hope to claim Jemina need to be cunning, protective and skilled warriors. This is her home, and she knows every inch within our village. If she wanted, she could hide within indefinitely, even from her own family. If someone invaded, we have little doubt she would be safe until help arrived. Yet her husbands will take her somewhere where she doesn't even know the village boundaries. If in danger there, it would be imperative for her new family to locate her and lead her to safety without delay." Leodon folded his arms. Though at least twenty or more cycles older than any of the men competing for his daughter's hand, he was fit and seasoned as warriors went. Crossing him in battle would be daunting.

"Somewhere within this village, our daughter hides. As a village born female, especially an unwed daughter of marriage age, she would be pursued by evildoers as the rarest prize of any community. Know this. She will not be found within any family unit. If this really was an attack, she would not want to endanger other families. Jemina awaits the first triad to locate her and transport her to the healer's compound, where, if she had been hurt during an actual attack, treatment would be available." The older man paused, waiting for the men who would compete to take in his words.

Then he continued, "Step outside of our border during your search, and you will not be allowed to return." He did not mince words. "Our daughter's first home will always be here. If for some reason your village cannot protect her, she will always return to us. As such, you need to know our village limits as well as you know your own."

Hendrix dared to speak. "Are there any limits on what a triad may do in pursuit of Jemina?"

"Harm her in any way," Leodon roared, "and you will not be given a chance to leave this land alive. Any more questions?" Stepping back, the younger man did not open his mouth again.

Once more, Jemina's father continued, "Warriors, find a portion of land to review your course of action. Since there is no real threat, you will be allowed no weapons. Your goal is simple. Find our daughter and bring her to the healer's compound. The triad to do so will be awarded the point. The horn will sound when it is time for you to begin this quest."

Glancing around, Aras finally located young Finnigan in a high tree. The child was clutching his horn and trying to remain out of sight. Without cluing the other triads of the boy's position, Aras nudged Anders and Loinbard. Finnigan gave his three new friends a big smile.

Loinbard tried to see if the child could provide them any assistance while his mates blocked him from view in case the other triads should look their direction. It was a needless precaution as the other triads were occupied formulating their own plans. Besides, the only person watching them closely was Ellias.

"Did you have any further instruction to give us, sir?" Aras asked upon noticing Jemina's oldest father studying them.

"Only that each triad will have an official observer to ensure nothing unexpected occurs while the competition is underway. Darnish has stationed himself close to the only triad to yet challenge our patience, namely the other Konrad crew. Leodon is thirsty for the blood of Hendrix and Johan, so he claimed rights to supervise their journey. I mean to make sure my daughter is not compromised by the affection she obviously holds for you three. You may have staked your official claim on her, but no wedding has been celebrated. Until then, there will be no exchange of seed with Jemina. I will slice off any organ trying to deliver such." Ellias was gleefully polishing off his sword as he made that comment.

Loinbard walked over to share what he learned, but seeing one of the fathers there, he forged innocence. "Blessed morning, sir. Do you have any more rules we need to be privy to before the challenge starts?"

"Speak freely, brother," Anders said. "Ellias will be joining us on our quest. As a warrior, he no doubt knows triads use any and all avenues of information before heading off to do battle. Battle was a poor word choice…" Always diplomatic, he tried to clarify himself.

"But a good analogy," Ellias pointed out with a smile. "You are battling for my daughter's hand. So long as no seed is being exchanged, I am solely a silent witness to your progress." Lifting his sword, he inspected his work, before working to shine another section.

Loinbard chose his words carefully. "I suspect we should begin our efforts on the north side of the village." His blue eyes darted to where Finnigan hid to add credibility to his information.

"The boy doesn't know where his sister truly hides," Ellias said in an even tone. "Not even her fathers know, though I would not be surprised if her mother and new sister-in-law are aware of more details. If villages allowed women to form triads, I fear they would outwit many of their male counterparts. Their seemingly illogical ideas are harder to predict, and therefore, impossible to prepare for."

"For a silent observer, one might think you are offering advice yourself," Loinbard suggested. "Admit it, sir, you know we are the best triad in this competition. You want us to win."

"I want my grandchildren conceived after their mother's wedding, not before," Jemina's oldest father said as he returned the sword to its holder. "I see you have already stowed your weapons in a safe place. It pleases me to know you respect the details of Leodon's rules. Did you notice the south side of the village is cloudy today? It casts shade which would help conceal that which seeks to be unseen."

"I propose we start our search on the south end," Anders announced with a smile. Ellias nodded slightly, signifying he thought such a plan was wise.

An ear-piercing blare interrupted Aras as he prepared to offer his suggestion of how to proceed. Turning, he saw Finnegan standing on a branch of the tree where he once hid. With one hand, he held the leaves out of his way, and the other held the horn to his lips. Dashing in that direction, Aras shouted for the boy to mind his balance. Behind him, Anders, Loinbard and Ellias raced toward the tree, too, but they were too late to stop the boy from losing his footing and falling. Aras reached up high to catch the boy, swinging him down and in a wide arc to help burn off some of the energy his tiny body had gained during the drop.

He ended up on the grass, cradling the giggling boy. "If Jemina was half as wild as this one when she was a child," Aras told Ellias in a winded voice, "you are to be praised for keeping her alive to see her wedding day."

12

Smiley's Devotion

They tried to talk him out of it, but Aras was sure his plan was sound. While Anders and Loinbard, and their shadow Ellias, headed directly for the south side of the village, he raced back to the center of the community. One of the seasoned warriors who had been charged with watching his triad during their stay in the village pursued him. It became clear where he was heading; the man stopped hiding his pursuit and made his presence known. Aras realized the man was likely thinking he meant to try searching for Jemina in some of the family units that lined the area.

"She will not be found in any of these dwellings," the older stranger warned, his voice deadly low. He was making no effort to hide his duty to protect the village from this outsider. His hand rested on his sword ready to attack if Aras dared to try entering any of the homes. From the dark shades of the Urijah colors the warrior was clad in, Aras wondered if the man was a powerful leader in the village, possibly even an elder. The Konrad warrior quickly dismissed the notion. It was hard to reconcile the image of an elder being tasked with this man's current obligation to watch over visitors to their land.

He should be ashamed, but it did please Aras to note the older, fit warrior running beside him was out of breath as they raced around the building until they reached where he was heading. Youth did have its advantages. Pulling a bit of meat from a pocket in his pants, Aras slowed down and approached a closed off area carefully. "I would be a fool to try making entrance into any of your family units."

The man was satisfied with the response and arrogantly dipped his jaw with approval. "You understand I would likely kill you for such an insult?"

"Actually, I believe I could hold my own against you at the moment, sir. I mean no disrespect, but you are quite exhausted from our recent foot race to this location, otherwise you would likely do me great harm. I believe any husbands inside any family unit I dare to enter would make quick work of spilling my blood with an arsenal of weapons lining the walls directly by the entrance."

"How do you know about the cache of weapons inside the family units?" The warrior was more indignant about that knowledge than the earlier comment about his exhaustion.

"Given that my own fathers have their armaments lining the interior walls of our family unit back in the village of Konrad, it was a logical conclusion. Trust me, sir. I do not seek an early death, only an extra advantage in the challenge Leodon set forth." Aras turned his attention back to what brought him to the center of the village.

"Hello, Smiley. I see someone has tied you up again. What a shame, too. It's a nice day to run free, isn't it?" The hound lapped up the treat being offer before he jumped up to rest his huge, muddy front paws on Aras' solid chest. With devotion, Smiley licked his scruffy face.

The Konrad warrior scratched under the dog's chin, earning more favor. "I bet you want to play today. Isn't that right, boy? Shall we find your mistress to see if she wants to run free with us?" Aras carefully unknotted the rope that kept the beast tethered in place. Then he wrapped a bit of the leash around his large palm and nudged Smiley forward. "Go, boy; find Jemina. If you help my triad win this challenge, I will be proud to call you my pet when we wed your mistress."

The dog darted out, pulling Aras behind him. Laughing, he turned back to witness the Urijah guard grimacing at the prospect of running another step. His next words were given respectfully. "I am fairly certain we are heading to the south side of the village, sir. If you chance to fall behind, that is the likely place you will find us again. My triad and I have a secret signal. You have no doubt already figured it out since you have watched us like the eagles from above since we crossed your village border. Just in case you have not concluded what the signal is, listen for the sound of a dove."

The Urijah warrior gave him an approving look. "Tis true, I have studied you three meticulously. Do not boast of it, but all nine triads guarding the competitors favor your group. Word of how you defended young Finnigan has not gone unnoticed. As for your signal, one coo of a dove is your marker, two is for the one called Anders and your blood brother gives off three. But know you my signal when I change shifts with my own triad?"

"Where do you think we got the idea for our bird calls?" Aras offered back. "You are the leader of your group, and one call of a mighty eagle means you have arrived to take over the duty of watching over us, or should I say me."

Off they went, stride for stride. They passed Hendrix's triad, which was heading to the north side of the village. The other Konrad triad was heading west. Nearing the south, Aras stopped to take in every detail around him. Hunting ground lay to the right of them. Somewhere within the thick foliage was an unmarked line dividing the area into Urijah region and the outside. If they had to enter in there, Aras knew he would need to be extra attentive to where the village warriors patrolled as a safeguard for not stepping out of bounds.

To his left, hills dotted the area, making clear visibility impossible. They would most likely find her there, he concluded. Jemina would likely avoid the forest if either of the Konrad triads were close by. But if the Finn men were near, she would transfer to the hunting region and try luring them out of bounds. She did not seem to mind Crosby, but Hendrix and Johan were a different matter. Jemina did not trust them any more than Aras did. He was thankful for her solid instinct on such matters.

Giving off the soft call of a dove, he started toward the hills. Anders returned the signal immediately indicating he and Loinbard where already searching the hilly area. Smiley put his nose to the ground for a moment before tugging straight ahead. Giving the dog his lead, Aras trusted the animal had caught Jemina's sweet scent.

The other members of his triad appeared at Aras' side. Ellias gestured to the man following close behind, no doubt conveying his acceptance of the transfer of duty to watch over the triad. The watchman slipped back out of sight. Smiley stopped a few times, before he moved slowly between trees and patches of tall boulders, as if something was confusing him. One moment the animal was sure his mistress was up ahead in one direction, only to switch to another suddenly.

"He is not one of the healer's beasts," Anders said as they followed closely behind the dog. "He was not bred for tracking. Given his odd number of teeth and toes, he might not be able to distinguish Jemina's scent from all the other smells lingering in the area."

Aras refused to give up hope. He placed tremendous faith in Smiley's awareness of his mistress. Anything Jemina touched would attract him. At the very least, the leader of the Konrad-Finn triad was certain their bride's smell lingered in whichever path the hound led them. Maybe Jemina had seen their approach and was purposely confusing the animal?

"Find her, boy!" he urged the dog on. "Don't let Jemina hide from us." He gave the dog a bit more rope length to search ahead.

Smiley pawed at the ground again, before howling and dashing to a small cluster of trees ahead. Loinbard gasped and pointed to where the hound was heading. "Well, Creator in the heavens above. I think I just saw a flash of the dress our sweet bride wore this morning."

Aras could not contain his excitement. He gave a shout of victory and set Smiley free. The hound reached the tree in question in a few bounds, long before any of the men following him could get there. It did not surprise any of them when the dog leapt high against the trunk and started tugging at the hem of the first-generation clothing they had seen Jemina wearing earlier. But his growling and sudden attack did astonish everyone.

His heart in his throat, Aras doubled his pursuit and wrestled the hound away from the tiny woman the animal had pulled from the tree. "What is wrong with you?" he shouted at the dog, tying him safely to another tree. Calling back to his triad, he prayed all was well. "Is Jemina badly injured?" Dear Creator, he prayed silently as he headed back to the prone figure being attended to by Anders and Ellias.

Loinbard answered. "It wasn't Jemina. It's the city bride her brother and his triad claimed. She's losing a fair amount of blood, brother. I fear she might be a bleeder."

The ringing in Aras' ears nearly made him fall to his knees. The words city bride and bleeder filled him with terror unlike any other fear he had encountered since reaching manhood. Giannis could die because of him. He had insisted on using the hound to track down Jemina. The city bride was wearing the dress Jemina had worn that very morning, her scent no doubt clinging to every fiber. When Smiley traced the smell to the other woman, he must have attacked when the person he encountered was not his beloved mistress.

"We've got to get her to the healer's compound," Anders said, tearing off the bottom of his shirt and binding up Giannis calf where the dog had bitten down.

"My husbands will be upset with me," the city bride moaned. "I ruined Leodon's mother's dress. Jael insisted it was unwise to help his twin in this challenge, but I was certain there would be no harm. I was only meant to help distract the competing triads by leading them one way while she headed another. I didn't see the dog coming and it must have sensed my fear."

Ellias lifted his new daughter-in-law in his strong arms. "I will deliver her to the healer. Swear to me that you will show nothing but respect to Jemina in my absence."

Anders and Loinbard did not hesitate, but Aras went to stand directly in front of Ellias. "It is my duty to bring Giannis to the healer. My actions caused this injury."

"I cannot halt this challenge for you, son. If you stop seeking Jemina now, the win will go to another group." The older man was unflinching in his words. "After what happened last time, Leodon was careful to set the rules for this match."

"My triad will continue searching in my absence. I bear responsibility for this damage. As such, I will not continue in the competition until Giannis is out of danger. Continue following my team, sir. You can trust me to get your daughter-in-law the treatment she requires. You have my word on it." Aras waited patiently. After careful consideration, Jemina's father eased Giannis into his arms.

"What should we do with the hound?" Anders inquired. "I do not think it is wise to use him to help track down Jemina now."

"I will return later to get Smiley and return him to where he belongs." Aras called over his shoulder. Then he spoke toward a bush up ahead. "Would you rush ahead and tell the healer to prepare for our arrival, sir. I prefer not to waste any time waiting for Dalia to gather her supplies once Giannis reaches the compound." The loud sound of an eagle call assured Aras his request was being honored.

"It is ironic," Giannis told him with a weak smile. "You have to take me to the healer because this if the first day my husbands did not feel the need to guard me now that the third claiming is complete."

He did not falter one step as he carried her, praying to the Creator for speed and divine intervention. "I will personally find your mates once you are safe and ensure they rush to your side."

Few words passed between Dalia and him when they arrived. The healer was focused on her job. Several cups of a healing herbal tea were forced down Giannis' throat before the strip of cloth binding the wound could be unfastened. Even with the direct pressure the bandage had provided, large amounts of blood still seeped from the ripped flesh. She quickly applied more bandages, giving Aras a grim look.

He nearly roared with anguish. How long had he fought this very event from coming to pass? A fragile, city bride lay before him, the life-giving blood pouring out of her because of him. Turning away from the two women, he slammed his fist against a bare patch of wall. The cases holding the healer's carefully maintained jars gave a protest at the vibration his action sent across the wall.

Rounding on the healer he demanded she prevent this needless death. "Go to the city and get the necessary fruit to save her."

His words rattled her, spoken aloud for anyone who came inside the compound to hear. She rushed to seal the entrances before acknowledging the command. "Lower your voice, son of

Ryder, Wolf and Kai. You above all others should understand the price to be paid for such an action."

"Absolutely," he bellowed, "I know the price. My family has paid your damn price. My baby sister was your price. One day soon the whole Creator forsaken city will pay a price, too. Save this innocent woman's life!"

"I would if I could!" she raged back at him. "Don't think for a moment that we healers are unaffected by this awful system. We live among you, remember, caring for those most in need. If we had any real control, changes would be made, exceptions allowed. We mourn each loss alongside the villages, doing our best to sway the priestesses in the city to modify their original agreement. It has been futile. Without the price to be sacrificed, they will not provide the life-giving fruit."

Aras' eyes darted to the jars lining the wall. The whole damn lot of priestesses acted as if they deserved Creator status, passing final judgment over life and death matters. He started to rip the cases from the walls to show them all his frustration when a crazy notion of one way to outmaneuver the system came to him.

"How many pups can you harvest from one of these vials, healer?" He held one aloft and she looked concerned with his tampering with her system.

"Do you honestly wish to discuss my hound breeding system now?" Dalia asked, working to make Giannis comfortable as she faded in and out of consciousness. "Three, maybe four offspring is a likely average. How could such knowledge help you, son of Konrad?"

He turned around and the cabinet shook as he slammed it with his palm. After a few seconds to calm himself, Aras turned and demanded the healer provide him with an empty jar. His request was fulfilled and he snatched the container before taking his leave. "Continue to do what you can for Giannis. I may be able to honor the damn price your priestess needs."

Aras returned later; the once empty vial now half full of a

white substance. He held it up for Dalia to examine. "Take this to your city leader. Offer it in exchange for the healing fruit."

She watched him warily as she would a crazed patient under her care. He could see the fear in her face and saw her reach for a syringe. Probably a concoction used to put people to sleep while being sewed up, Aras decided. "Do not concern yourself with my sanity, healer. I have not gone mad, just desperate. This is the only way I can conceive for making the payment necessary to save her life."

When Dalia took the container, he shoved her away and walked over to check Giannis' breathing. The bandage around her leg was nearly soaked now. Time was running out. "The prize you hold may not be a newborn daughter, but the potential is there. Even if my seed results in three sons and only one daughter, the price will be met."

"You filled this jar… do you understand what you are suggesting, son of Konrad? Truly understand the ramifications of what you are suggesting?" The healer examined his reaction carefully before shaking her head in resolution. "Such an offer has never been tried, but I will do my best to broker the exchange. You must stay here and watch over her," Dalia ordered, pointing to the city bride. "I will return with all haste."

The healer touched a secret section of floor near the far wall. A trapdoor opened below and wide stairs led to the second level of the compound. Aras rushed to follow her so he could watch as she gained access to the third level; it was too late. The opening closed and he could only surmise what happened next.

From what his fathers had explained, the healer in their village had a hidden exit under the heavy bed where mothers labored. A secret knob caused the bed to shift positions to show a clandestine tunnel below. The narrow path led underground linking the room with the city. A small opening in the rock by the wall there allowed a newborn baby to be handed over and a life-saving seed to be returned.

It seemed to be a long time before the healer reappeared. By then, a commotion outside the compound suggested Giannis' mates had arrived and were trying to gain access to the first level. Between the two of them, Aras and Dalia managed to get the seed down the city bride's throat. Now only time would prove if it was too little, too late.

"I trust this matter will be kept in confidence, son of Konrad." Dalia started for the entrance so the husbands could be given access. "Your sacrifice shocks me. You have already lost so much because of the travesty of the priestesses' actions, two sisters if I am not mistaken…"

"And a mother, nearly two," he replied, hatred seething from every sound he uttered.

"Yet you just offered another generation of innocent lives to them. Any daughters produced from your seed will never know you. I do not even care to think what will become of any male offspring which results in the use of your seed."

Beside Aras, Giannis started moaning, her voice noticeably stronger than just moments before. A smile crept across his lips. "First, I did what was necessary to save an innocent life. The Creator in heaven will no doubt forgive the desperate measures I was forced to take."

Dalia nodded her agreement. "It was an honorable sacrifice. One, few would consider, much less follow through with for someone else's bride."

"Secondly, I promised myself none of my children would ever end up in the city, even if I had to remain a virgin to ensure it. My seed would never be planted inside a city inhabitant."

The healer's face grew pale. "You said you understood the ramifications of what you offered in exchange for the life-giving fruit? The priestess will use the sample you provided to breed as many offspring as possible, even cloning the resulting children if necessary."

A sarcastic grin covered Aras' face. "Is the value of pups so high in the city, then?" He watched her begin to reason out what he was suggesting. "Did you really think I would offer up my own seed to the evil people who run the city? After everyone I have already lost because of them? I do hope you collected more than one sample from the alpha gray hound whose semen you just exchanged with the priestess. I would hate to be responsible for your line of tracking hounds to dwindle because of me."

13

Another Price to be Paid

Jemina made no effort to hide the disdain she felt for having to sit so close to Johan and Hendrix at the evening meal. How much humiliation would she have to bear because of one, poor miscalculation? Her hearing was superior to many. Jemina counted on such when necessary. It had given her an advantage over knowing who was heading her direction in the second challenge. It also flushed her out, causing Crosby of all warriors to stumble upon her.

The witless man had gotten separated from his triad and was on the opposite side of the village from them. She had been tempted to rush off so the win would not go to the Finn triad, but as luck would have it, a Urijah warrior witnessed the entire event and sent her back to do the honorable thing. Why did there always seem to be witnesses around lately?

Her brother and his triad had begun their work on protecting the village wall today, since the third claiming of their bride was complete. Giannis' accident had sent a shock wave through the village, and various people were doing their best to locate the husbands so they could go to their wife in her moment of need.

Hendrix used the guise of reaching for a platter of meat to

try moving his chair closer to Jemina. She automatically moved further away, only to have Johan crowd her in on the other side. Slipping her dagger from a hidden sheath on her thigh, she made a production of stabbing it deeply into the slab of beef on his plate.

"My apologies," she quipped boldly. "I almost cut you. Maybe it would be best to put a bit of distance between our plates for your own safety." Her steel eyes locked on him as she extracted the sharp blade and laid it beside her plate, ready to access it again if she felt so inclined. Johan retreated but an inch or so, but Jemina took pride in his withdrawal.

Ellena moved around the table, coming to stand between Hendrix and her daughter. Using her small frame as leverage, Jemina's mother found a way to push herself forward. Soon she was sharing her daughter's seat. The village bride smiled at her mother's protection, only to realize someone had done the same on the other side, insulating her from Johan's presence.

"Giannis?" Jemina shrieked with joy. "Are you feeling stronger? I am so sorry you were wounded trying to aid me today. I know my brother will never forgive me for encouraging your participation, but I pray one day you will find it in your heart to pardon me."

"There is nothing to forgive." The city wife smiled. Her next words were directed at Johan. "Would you be so kind as to move your chair over a bit. It's so crowded."

The soldier complied, but his expression was dark and promised retaliation for taking away his right to dine beside Jemina. His triad had been the first to locate her, after all. Konrad's men had been allowed to dine beside her after their win. "You missed the end of today's challenge while you were in the healer's care. Shall we detail how the Village of Finn claimed the victory?" he sneered.

Ellena stole his attempt to brag. "Jemina caught wind of your injury, Giannis. In her haste to rush to your side, she lost her footing on the branch she was perched on and fell. Crosby was below her at the time, and she landed on top of him."

"His body did provide me with a nice cushion to break my fall," Jemina added. "I never thanked you for that kindness, sir." She graced him with a full smile. Across from her, Crosby still looked confused by the events, which led to the Village of Finn being awarded the second win. He was probably wondering if the Creator had dropped the village bride in his lap as a sign, they were meant to win her hand.

"Wife, care you to explain how you ended up sitting here?" Jael appeared from nowhere, his triad at his side. "You claimed you only needed a moment of privacy when you asked to be excused from our table."

"And I did, husband. I wanted a moment alone with my dear, new sister." Giannis seemed to be trying to keep her tone even. "Soon she will leave our home and any chance of mending bruised feelings will be gone. Sit, dear mates. Crosby, would you mind moving a few chairs down so my husbands can sit across from us. As Jemina's twin, it is important for Jael to enjoy what little time he has left with his sister."

Before Jael could object outright, his two triad brothers shoved aside Crosby. The Konrad triad had already moved down to allow for the newcomers. Aras, Anders and Loinbard noted the blatant distaste of the Urijah when they regarded Hendrix and Johan. Now that they were no longer fairly secluded with their bride for most of the day, they had probably heard much about those who competed for Jemina's hand.

Realizing he was outnumbered; Jael reluctantly took a seat across from his bride. His eyes bored into Johan first and then Hendrix until each uncomfortably moved their seats over. Ellias appeared out of nowhere, two chairs in arm. Now the three ladies could sit easily without perching on a single stool.

"Our guests at the other table will be wondering about our absence," Jael said in a low voice.

"My parents and siblings are too busy enjoying tonight's dessert, brother," Chaim offered. "We won't be missed for a brief visit."

Moshe, the third member of Jael's triad reached over to lay claim to Crosby's goblet of wine and helped himself to a healthy gulp. "Our wife has already accepted the blame for putting herself in danger. Are we to shame her in front of your family by acting so rudely?" Jemina heard his low sanction meant for her twin's ears alone. It made her wince. Her foolish actions had caused strife among the new family unit.

"Tis true, Giannis has accepted her responsibility." Jemina's twin brother locked eyes with her now. "She is new here, unaware of the dangers which lurk. I no longer seek her remorse. The wound on her ankle will serve as a lesson against being led into future rash actions."

Swallowing hard, Jemina found the courage to admit her fault. Her beautiful, new sister could have been seriously injured today. Praise the Creator above for planting Aras nearby to protect her. She had little doubt Hendrix and Johan would never have given up the challenge to help Giannis. Crosby might have tried, but would have gotten lost or caused greater damage.

"You are right not to hold a grudge against your innocent wife. Someone else is solely responsible for today's accident. That person alone should face the consequences, brother. Announce the punishment to be meted out, and it will be accepted."

"I am no longer responsible for correcting you, sister, now that I have formed my own family unit. That falls to the triad that heads your unit. Our fathers have lacked the heart to address your poor choices from your very birth. I pray your husbands will learn to tame your wilder traits without bending your brilliant mind and skill as a warrior." Jael had turned toward where Aras, Loinbard and Anders sat when he gave those words. Only two of the three remained at the table though.

Aras had moved to stand directly behind Jemina. His hands

on her shoulders, his voice resolute, he said, "Your sister is not to blame for Giannis' wound. That blame lies solely with me. She did not realize I had been sneaking bits of food to her pet hound, winning his trust to use as an extra advantage if a challenge arrived where I needed him. Had I not freed the dog and set him on the trail of her scent, none of this would have happened. Even Smiley is not at fault. He protects his mistress. I put him in a position where an innocent startled him and his animal instinct took over."

The three men watched Aras carefully. Their wife understood the threat that passed between them. Giannis started to protest, but Jael motioned for her to remain quiet. Jemina tried to intervene next, but Aras' fingers tightened against her skin, so she, too, kept silent. "May I suggest we take up this matter later tonight after the ladies have turned in? My triad conveniently beds down in your meeting area."

Loinbard and Anders began to take their feet to join Aras, knowing what his words meant. Punishment within the villages was meted out with an iron hot cane across the back of the offenders. As his brothers, they were agreeing to accept payment for his action as their own. "My brothers are in no way responsible for the wound Giannis received. I alone will stand before you ready to make amends." Aras stalled their action. Both men gave Aras a challenging eye.

"Agreed," Jael said. His eyes met Loinbard and Anders. "Your brother already paid a part of the price by leaving the games to make sure our wife reached the healer. The original count will be reduced as such." A pleasant smile soon replaced the censuring expression Jemina's twin bore from before. "Some good did come from the entire catastrophe."

The hands on her shoulders stopped her from rising, but Jemina refused to be quieted. "What does it mean, 'the original count will be reduced as such', brother? If anyone is to bear the weight of this punishment, it shall be me. Aras is not from this village. Only a family member may accept the lot of the offender, namely me. I will not allow him to do so in my stead."

Aras bent low and ordered her to stop speaking. "The matter is closed. If you have any respect for me as a man and a warrior, do not shame me before all who share this meal." As if trusting her regard for him to cease her protest, he walked back to his seat to continue his meal. Her brother's triad clearly valued Aras' actions. Though the punishment had yet to be carried out, all was forgiven concerning the issue.

"There was one glorious outcome from today's events." Ellena broke the heavy silence. "Our dear Giannis is clearly not a bleeder." Aras stiffened, as did his blood brother.

"But I am a bleeder. Most virgin births are such," Giannis countered. "Inside the city walls, I needed vast amounts of the seeds from the Tree of Life throughout my existence. I did not realize they were in such short supply here until Aras tried to make your healer fetch some for me. I heard his angry words when she did not follow his orders immediately. Though the confusion of going in and out of an uneasy sleep muddled my thinking about most things going on around me, I am sure Aras ensured my recovery by getting the seed for me."

Ellena vaguely recalled the tree her daughter-in-law spoke of from her time in the city, though it was many cycles ago. "Some of the women I worked alongside of required the seeds from the tree you speak of, but I was lucky not to be a bleeder. I never paid much attention to the topic, because the tree was always available. It was only when I came here that I realized it was difficult to harvest. I was unaware Dalia had such a plant here in our village. Until this very moment, I have never heard of such a tree being located outside of the walls of the city."

Aras cursed himself. The secret was in jeopardy because he had spoken too freely in front of those outside of his family unit. He had to repair the damage without doing more harm. "The body acts strangely when someone is hurt, Giannis. The mind tries to help us deal with the pain forced upon us, especially when we lose vast amounts of blood. Your past experiences with the city's use of some mysterious seeds of life no doubt took over your thinking. Your brain probably wanted the proven solution such a cure was close at hand and believed it was coming quickly."

Giannis looked puzzled now by his explanation. "But… I was certain you fought with Dalia over providing me with the seed." Shaking her head, she pondered more hazy memories. "Of course, I also thought I heard you offer up three sons and a daughter from your own family to the city priestess," she giggled. "No men are allowed inside the city walls, so I recalled thinking it was an odd promise." Now she laughed gaily, no longer fretting over the false memories he suggested she had of the seeds.

"Share what makes you so gleeful, wife," Jael asked playfully. "We all could use a good laugh to ease the tension."

"Aras must be speaking the truth because my memories are quite ridiculous now that I think about them. In my haze, I thought I heard him demand the necessary seed to save me. Then I was sure Dalia insisted there was a price to pay, but he didn't have any newborn female babes to offer up for the seed." Clutching her stomach, Giannis tried to gasp for air.

Aras, too, was void of fresh oxygen as he held his breath, powerless to stop her as she shared a secret his family had guarded for cycles now. His blood sister's life hung in the balance suddenly. Would his careless actions cost his childhood family unit to lose all hope of her return? Loinbard tensed beside him, anger taking hold of his expression as well.

"Then Aras gave Dalia some gray hound's seed so the city women could have babies who excel at smelling, and she happily retrieved the seed from the Tree of Life for me," Giannis finished saying. "What a ridiculous notion! We don't even have hounds within the city's limits."

14

Back on Track

Anders covered Jemina's lips with his callused hand and pulled her back out of view before the others in the meeting area could notice her presence. He whispered in her ear. "He will not forgive your interference, Jem. Allow him the honor of reclaiming his pride, or Giannis' injury will weigh heavily on his heart for cycles to come."

Loinbard stood beside his brother. Aras slowly removed his shirt and tossed it aside. Jael, Chaim and Moshe circled him, laying out the charges against him for him to respond to, so the punishment could proceed. "Do you alone take responsibility for our wife's wound, son of Konrad?" Chaim, the rightful leader of the triad, asked.

"I do," Aras replied, an expression of deep resolve taking over his face. "I agree to accept the consequences so I can know this sinful stain is released from my soul."

"But you do not even know the number of strikes to be inflicted for your actions, yet do readily accept the price?" Moshe seemed incredulous by the calm the man they circled showed.

"Though my time in your village has been brief, I have learned a lot about your people and the honor they demonstrate.

Jemina is a brave, skilled woman because of her childhood within these boundaries. Her fathers and mother are honest, faithful followers of Urijah's code of ethics. As their son, I know Jael will share their tendencies. Since he claims you two as brothers in his triad, my trust extends to you as well. I gladly accept any number given as a just punishment to restore my honor and cleanse me of this sin."

Jael passed judgment. "Three strikes are warranted, one for each of Giannis' husbands."

"I seek to take a share of my brother's portion." Loinbard made known his intent to accept at least one of the prescribed strikes in Aras' stead.

"Before we consider your offer," Moshe interrupted, "hear out the full sentence. Three strikes are required, but one has already been paid. By bringing our wife to the healer, you bore responsibility for your actions. The first strike is no longer needed."

Chaim spoke next, "By leaving the challenge Leodon set forth, you gave up a chance to claim a victory to honor your responsibility for getting our wife needed aid. For this reason, the second strike is considered paid in full."

"The final strike will wipe clean any lingering stain of regret you may harbor, brother." Jael picked up a red, hot poker that rested in a nearby fire. "Are you still willing to pay the price, Aras, son of Konrad?"

He gave his back to Jemina's twin in reply. Her scream of outrage was muffled by Anders' hand as a solid blow caught Aras across the top of his shoulders. Tears poured down her face at the pain the man she loved endured. But Aras simply remained quiet, letting the blow dissipate through his body. Only then did he walk away, grabbing his shirt as he did so, for a moment alone to collect his thoughts.

Hendrix and Johan had watched the entire scene from their resting spot on the raised platform near the center of the meeting area. Satisfied to see one of their competitors suffer, they exchanged looks of approval. "I bet Aras will think twice before crossing any of you again now that he knows what follows such an insult," Hendrix told Jael.

Instead of accepting the offhanded compliment, Jemina's twin gave the Finn warrior a look of repulsion. "I count Aras and, therefore his triad, as my brothers now. It is human to make miscalculations. Owning up to errors, even unintentional ones, is part of being a man."

Chaim moved toward the center of the area, Moshe with him, but the latter remained silent while their leader explained. "What we do find offensive, son of Finn, is a pompous group of outsiders daring to scatter their belongings along the hallowed ground used to celebrate the life and death of descendants of Urijah.

"Or the disrespect of strangers making their beds on sacred land..." Jael said. As one, his triad stepped forward to the base of the platform and waited. No further words were necessary. Moshe held one of the pokers that were stored near the fire pit. He slapped it against his hand, lowering his face to regard the men above with disdain. Johan and Hendrix reluctantly started collecting their belongings to relocate. They ordered a naïve Crosby to do the same.

A long time passed before Anders released his hold on Jemina. By then, her brother's triad had departed and the other competitors were gaining their sleeping rolls to turn in. She wasted no time seeking out Aras where he stood twenty feet away. The soft glow of the fire hid his back in shadows, but she could still imagine the ugly scar that was left behind in the angry poker's wake.

He must have heard her coming, because he turned in her direction and found her throwing herself into his arms. He stroked her back, trying to soothe her sobbing. "You do not belong here, Jem. I would have preferred you not witness my shame. But know you one thing, it pleases me that you did not intervene. It means you respect me as a warrior and mate. I am humbled to have earned such an honor."

"My respect for you is deep, but I would have screamed my head off given the chance." She wept into his warm, massive chest, which was still bare. Jemina inhaled his strong scent, his pleasant smell tinged with scorched flesh now. She found strength in the smooth, hard lines of his rib cage, tracing the area with her fingers. "Anders held me fast, not letting me rush to your side. Oh, Aras, it breaks my heart to see you suffer. I would rather face the punishment myself."

"It was not your punishment to accept," he scolded her. Anders and Loinbard appeared and the four walked a bit farther from the meeting area so they could be assured of privacy. "How did you manage to slip off into the night, village daughter? If your family unit is in any way as protective as mine, your fathers should have been able to intervene any escapes."

"It is my family's bonding night," she explained, a shameful look tinging her cheeks a delightful red. Husbands and wives were afforded one night of guaranteed privacy each week. Any children were cared for by relatives to allow for procreation purposes. "My siblings are off at one of my fathers' family member's unit."

"You were not expected to join them there?" Loinbard teased, taking a seat, and resting his back against a tall tree.

"I may have given the impression I was staying at a different family member's dwelling so I could escape Finnegan's pitiful attempts at blowing his horn." She giggled and they all smiled at her mischievous glow. "My brother takes his duty to announce each challenge quite seriously. I would gladly make the awful instrument vanish otherwise."

Aras helped her find a clean patch of grass to rest on before he and Anders sat down. "If you were one of my children, Jem, I would make sure the consequences for leaving your home made you second guess any future attempts. As it is, I am sure your own fathers will want to take up the issue with you come sunrise."

She gave an impish grin. "Creator willing, they will never learn of my little act of disobedience. If necessary, I will sleep near Smiley until night is over. When my brothers return home, I will rise and rejoin their number, my parents being none the wiser."

"No less than three of your fathers' friends are observing our every move right now, my sassy Jem." Anders smiled, pulling her to rest on his lap. "Your parents will know of your transgressions. Even if the Urijah warriors do not tell, the three of us will."

"You would knowingly cause me trouble?" she pouted, cuddling against his strong chest. "I only snuck out to make sure Aras was safe. My intentions were pure."

The rumbling of his laughter sounded in her ear as Jemina relaxed. "I fear your husbands will have their hands full trying to keep you out of harm's way."

"But the three of you are up to the challenge," she murmured back. Her eyes growing heavy. "Do try not to lose any more of the challenges," she scolded Aras. "I cannot stomach another meal with those horrible men beside me."

"None of us enjoyed the sight either," Loinbard said, wanting his turn to share a few stolen touches with their chosen bride. He reached over to nudge her toward his firm legs. Removing his shirt, he covered her shoulders before starting to stroke her soft hair. "You wouldn't have any hints to give us an advantage over the others regarding the next event?" he teased.

"Finnigan helped Papa Darnish come up with tomorrow's game. He is positive Hendrix or Johan will disqualify themselves and be banished from the competition. How are you three with handling children?"

Aras, the warrior who had not flinched at a hot poker to the back, recoiled. "Children? What sort of challenge would involve sucklings? I have not changed a wee baby's underpants in many cycles, Jemina. Feeding one is even more foreign to me because my second mother breastfed her babes."

She giggled at his discomfort. "If you are going to be a father one day, you will need to help your devoted wife care for your children. But do not fret over such concerns at present. I speak of children a bit older than sucklings with dirty underpants or empty tummies. A new batch of fledglings is due to start training tomorrow. You will work with boys of twelve or fourteen cycles in age. Finnegan exposed my spying as they discussed the plan, and Darnish banned me from the ground level while they could finalize the rules. I believe he wishes to see what methods my potential mates would employ to prepare a new generation of warriors."

The sound of an eagle interrupted any further discussion. Aras got to his feet, pulling Anders, Jemina and finally Loinbard up. "We have been signaled to return our village princess to her family unit."

"Signaled by whom?" she demanded, not ready to part from their company.

"A tall, beast of a warrior with reddish gray hair and an impressive scar across his forehead.

"Grandfather Ian?" she paled. "That eagle's caw was from him. He won't tell my fathers about my behavior. He will see to my punishment himself. The leather belt which hangs across his waist is brutal."

Loinbard smiled at her dismay. He turned her toward the direction of her home and gave her a loud smack across the backside to start her moving. "You will face the consequences of your rash decision to put yourself in danger tonight, be it from your fathers or grandfathers."

"Or us," Aras applied three swift blows to her small fanny, nodding with approval when she gasped at the pain they caused. "We may not have a thick strap of leather at hand, but I think one of the spare pokers near the fire would help stress the foolishness of impulsive choices."

Jemina faced Anders, denying him access to her already throbbing bottom. "And to think I came here to support you three. Why would I even consider husbands who would dare to inflict pain upon a devoted, loving wife?"

Anders chuckled, dropping down to one knee and tugging her off balance. She ended up face down, his hand positioned above her ass. With a playful whisper, he suggested she project loud and clear so her grandfather would know she was paying the price for her poor judgment. As if she needed advice. His hard hand rained down on her poor, unprotected backside repeatedly.

Twenty of his unyielding blows had to equal the agony of the hot poker. She screeched and wiggled, trying to free herself. At one point, she looked up to beg Aras or Loinbard for assistance. She found them nodding with approval, even indicating Anders should not end the punishment too soon. Balling her hands, she pounded them into the ground. It would serve them right if she pulled the dagger from her thigh and cut a strip off their backsides.

A weary expression replaced her rebellious thoughts. She could never do lasting harm to any of these men, even the horrible brute bruising her ass. She adored each of them. Jemina took comfort in knowing they would never truly harm her, either. Even this correction, she had to admit, was not given in irritation. They sought to help her curb her more impulsive actions. Like Aras had said when he accepted the hot poker across his back, the punishment helped cleanse him of his sins. She melted against Anders, letting redemption wash over her.

Afterwards, Aras, Loinbard and Anders escorted her back to her grandfather Ian's home. Leodon's father thanked them for the courteous act before signaling for someone from inside to allow access to the first level. It was Aras who dared to push his luck. "In our villages, it is important to provide comfort after a correction is delivered to those under our care. May we kiss your granddaughter good night, sir? To ensure she knows this matter is done and will not be spoken of again?"

Blocking the entrance with his frame, the older warrior grunted, "Make it quick."

Jemina thought to turn her back on the three men before her, but in the end, she could not deny herself a chance to enjoy their more pleasant attentions. She walked to stand by Aras first, since he had been bold enough to put the question to her grandfather. Standing on tiptoes she, reached up to allow him access to her lips. He roughly yanked her into his arms, nearly knocking her off balance. His steel arms locked around her waist as he lifted her up and took possession of her mouth. His tongue demanded access, and she tilted her head back and allowed her lips to part. A loud cough sounded by the entrance, suggesting her grandfather's patience was wearing thin. She was back on her own feet again, but they were shaky at best.

Anders pulled her to him, bending her head up so he could get better access. His tongue did not merely explore her mouth, it sought to duel with her own. Light-headed now, she savored the thrill of his taste, different from Aras, but still intoxicating.

Loinbard came forward once she was freed again. He stared in her eyes as his lips moved down to cover her own. Her lids began closing but he ordered her to keep them wide. "I want to watch your reaction to my kiss, Jem. It pleases me to see your steel blue eyes go dark and wide with passion. You will be a wild lover when wed. I torture myself with that notion as I try to sleep."

She was shoved inside moments later, and Jemina's hand reached up to examine her swollen lips. Her grandfather, Ian frowned down at her, but she was too far lost in the glory of her lovers' kisses to notice. Her underclothes were damp, and she wished Aras was available to help change them.

15

Darnish's Challenge

Konrad-Finn Triad: 1 win

Finn Triad: 1 win

The anarchy taking place below them give Aras, Loinbard and Anders pause. Adolescents of varying ages and sizes ran about the training field unsupervised and feral. Taller, arrogant boys pushed younger counterparts down to the lower level, mocking their slight stature or weaker fighting skills. Wooden daggers and swords swung wildly around, without the least concern for accidently hitting an unsuspecting neighbor. A fair amount of fresh blood littered the ground.

Loinbard was the first to speak. "I would rather change suckling's underpants than waste time on this undisciplined lot."

"Are you so old that you have forgotten the thrill of finally being allowed to train as a fledgling, my new brother. I wager we all were as wild as these young boys when we took the field that first, official training season." Anders grimaced as a chubby child tripped over his own feet, falling over the edge of one level and landing on a smaller child below. He held his breath until the smaller child freed himself and extracted revenge with a mighty blow of his wooden sword. The sight filled him with pride for the young boy's courage.

The Finn warrior smiled with amusement suddenly. "Now I understand why mothers are not allowed to observe the training process. My orderly, tiny mother would be unable to stop herself from marching out there and taking away all the practice weapons being shoved around carelessly. Then she'd have all the boys sit in quiet, lined rows to await proper instruction."

"I prefer watching these future fighters in their own natural environment," Aras said as he glanced over the viewing stands at the mock battles taking place below. "It gives us a clean measure of each child we might have to deal with."

Hendrix and Johan were bored. Apparently, they assumed the challenge had nothing to do with the children, and the triads where merely waiting for the ground to become available for their task. The Finn warriors did not bother to waste time watching children play. Crosby took the time to catch up on his sleep in a shady corner of the viewing platform.

The other triad for Konrad observed the events going on below. They chuckled at some of the antics taking place on the field, discussing a few memories of their own first day of training. Aras heard them take bets on which of the boys would end up vanquished to the lowest level in the battle the children waged.

Tyler, the oldest of their group, saw great promise in some scruffy looking teenagers. The boys were not yet paired off, but he suggested the three of them would make an excellent team. Aras agreed with his observations, knowing he would no longer consider those children since the other triad had noticed them first.

Jemina came to stand close by, but her back was to them so as not to attract too much attention. "I spent more years on the training hills than any other fledgling," she said in a casual tone.

"Every cycle, a new set of fledglings appear, ready to begin their training. It was fun to watch them exhaust themselves showing off for their trainers. After a few cycles, I grew tired of watching the fresh recruits make fools of themselves. They were finally allowed to join the sessions but were unorganized and comical. It was more insightful to note what the warriors who would train them concentrated on as they watched the new recruits." She slanted her head to the right where a few strong warriors watched and discussed the events going on below.

Aras motioned for his brothers to inch closer to their chosen bride so they could learn more. "And what do they focus on, Jem? How can this chaos provide helpful information?" He asked in a low voice, his warm breath blowing strands of her hair aside. He took pleasure in the way she shivered slightly.

"It is never too early to note strong bonds and potential groups for determining effective teams for training purposes. Triads may not be formed for cycles to come, but clusters of fledglings will be quickly sorted into squads for drilling sessions. The men charged with leading the exercises are careful to seek as much information as they can before even calling a halt to the fun and giving their welcoming speech. Which boys work together? Which are too immature to realize alliances improve the odds? Which have been trained in fighting by fathers and which are unskilled in even the most basic fighting methods?"

She dared to glance back at the three men near her. Each was dressed in their village's colors. Sighing, Jemina wondered if there were three more attractive men in all of new earth. She imagined the few survivors from the war on old earth were much like Aras, Anders and Loinbard. Strong, wise, fit for protecting what was theirs. They would give her strong, skilled offspring.

"I can easily see flaws in that young boy, there. He reminds me a lot of Hendrix and Johan," she told them, pointing to a boy who flexed his muscles and fought dirty to maintain his position on the top level. "A knowledgeable trainer would quickly realize the potential for trouble with such arrogance. He would ensure the boy learn humility before moving to a higher position in the training class. Since you are unlikely to have much time to work with the children, it would be best to avoid spending too much effort on him or others like him. It will take cycles to break through his arrogance, if ever."

Anders gave her a smile, nudging his new brothers with pride in her wisdom. "If you were training this lot, which boys would you consider to have the best potential?"

She bent over the side for a better view, and Aras quickly grabbed hold of her slender hips to help maintain her balance. He pulled her further back and gave her a silent frown. Jemina had little doubt he would smack her backside if she dared to repeat the action. Since it was already sore from last night's secret visit, she felt it was best to heed his warning.

She waited until one of her fathers had moved farther out of hearing range before speaking. It pleased Jemina that her preferred triad listened to her advice. Had she earned their respect? They had gained hers.

"Established sets of children are no doubt best for the challenge Darnish has planned. They already know how to share duties and work effectively as a team. See that group of boys on the middle level? They are blood brothers. The two older brothers are strong enough to challenge for the top level, but they won't sacrifice their younger brother for the fleeting victory. They guard his back as he finds the courage to hold his ground and protect himself from those seeking to send him down to the lowest, weakest level. This gives him a chance to work on his sparring skills so they improve as a unit and can challenge for higher rank later on."

Loinbard asked about another group of boys near the top level on the side farthest from where they stood. "Those three children over there are cutthroat and wield a mighty wooden sword. They took out that larger set of boys by working together. Wouldn't they work just as well and be a better choice?"

"I noticed them as well," Anders said, a touch of bitterness in his tone. "Two of the three seem more united than the third. I have little doubt they will only allow him to join with them so long as it benefits their agenda. The moment it doesn't, they will turn on him without hesitation."

"Is that what Hendrix and Johan did to you?" Jemina touched his arm. "No wonder I am repulsed by them. Anyone who could insult you in such a way could never be a friend of mine."

Anders' face filled with a grin. "Do not be too harsh with their rejection of me. Had it not been for them, I would never have ventured here and joined forces with my new brothers. It was almost as if the Creator above planned each of our paths to lead us to this point in time. Aras, Loinbard and I have bonded closer in a few days than my old triad had in cycles of working together. We share a common rare gem."

Jemina recalled her many, vivid dreams. "I suspect the Creator knows our union would be a perfect fit." Dare she share her nighttime visions? They might think she was wanton and lose some of their respect because of her foolish, romantic notions.

Darnish summoned the candidates to where he stood. "It is time to announce the third challenge. At present, Konrad-Finn's men claim one victory. Finn's triad has the second. May the best set of men take a win from today's event. Below you will find the future warriors who will protect our village borders and the city wall. If any of you produce daughters, one of these boys could show up at your family unit to fight for the right to claim her as their bride.

"You have had a chance to observe what talents are present within the children, what skills they bring to the training fields and what deficits they need to work on improving. Each triad will be allowed to select three from the budding fledglings below. You will have two days to work with them, under our watchful observation, of course. At the end of that time, we will gather in the meeting area for a unique competition. This time, you will not be fighting for the win this challenge sets forth. The young charges you select will take the knowledge you provided them to earn you a glorious victory or shame in defeat."

"THEY KEEP FALLING OVER EACH OTHER," Anders complained. "I doubt we will have time to help them learn to move as one."

The youngest boy, a lad of twelve stopped training to glare at the Konrad-Finn warriors. "Untie the rope you have anchoring us together and we won't knock into each other as much."

Loinbard turned away, not wanting the boys to see his amusement. The three fledglings saw his broad shoulder's shake, and mistook his laughter for rage. A redheaded, older boy grabbed hold of the length of rope connected to his younger brother's ankle. He gave it a pull, sending the boy falling on his butt in reproach. "Show some respect, Usman. Do you want to get us beaten?"

Aras stepped forward and pulled the youngster back up. He regarded the three boys solemnly. "We do not beat those under our care," he sought to assure them. A reproachful sound echoed from the thick tree behind him. Hands on his hips, he swung around and walked over to spy Jemina perched behind a thick cluster of leaves.

"Tell that to my ass," she hissed down at him. Loinbard's laughter was uncontrollable now. Anders stepped between Aras and the boys to distract them.

"Do you truly consider that mild correction to be in line with a beating?" Aras demanded. When she finally admitted as much, he spoke again, "Interrupt our training session again without a helpful hint or suggestion, and I will pull you down from that tree, turn your backside as red as a hot poker and send you away. Do you understand me, young lady?"

Sticking her tongue out at him, she pulled the leaves in front of her body and hid from view. Shaking his head, he returned to the boys. "Listen carefully so I can explain Anders' suggestion to unite you with a rope at the ankles. You each are skilled at moving about, facing challenges ahead of you, and many from behind. Many grown fledglings take cycles to learn as much."

Usher, the oldest of the lot grinned boldly at the praise. "But we aren't working as an effective team?" He acknowledged with maturity well beyond his years.

"Two of you are," Anders interjected. "You and Ulices are masters of protecting your brother's back. You have been holding your own development in check, no doubt waiting for him to catch up to your own level."

"Our mom would not let us join the training field until he was ready," Ulices, who was probably Usher's twin explained. "She was worried his wild ways might cause him harm, and suggested it would be the brotherly thing to do. Our mother is a very persuasive woman, sirs. Besides, as aggravating as Usman may be, he has the makings of a great warrior one day. We mean to form a triad so we can service the city wall and claim a bride."

Aras tensed, knowing the folly such a plan meant, but unable to explain why. This was not the time or place to agonize over the family secret he guarded. "We know of Usman's skill. You two are not as observant. He is close, if not equal, to your ability to wield a weapon. It is time for you three to learn the task of working as one."

Anders took over the explanation and his new brothers walked over to position the fledglings. "You are no longer held back from perfecting your fighting skills. It is time to work on honing your talents. Yes, you need to protect the youngest, but don't let him fight your battles alone."

"Ha!" Usman smirked. "Told you. I am a mighty warrior. Stop sitting on your asses and fight alongside me. I am not a baby!"

Loinbard dropped to a knee so he was eye to eye with the youngest child. "You also need to learn how to work as a team, young man. You are so used to your brothers protecting your back that you are often vulnerable from behind." Nodding with understanding, the boy proudly boasted he could easily correct that fault. "But it is not your own back you need to protect, Usman. It is time to be equal to your brothers and protect them with as much dedication as they have you in the past. Can you do that?"

Aras addressed all three boys now. "You cannot protect a brother who is out of your reach. The rope helps train warriors to be attentive of where members of the triad are at all times. Soon you will not need it to help you gauge when the others stand or what challenges they are dealing with."

"But our father and his triad tell brave tales of their battles. They leave one member exposed, while the other two plan counter attacks from the side." Usher sought clarification.

It was Loinbard who clarified the point. "Yes, there will be times when you must move individually to address challenges your triad faces. When outside of the village, enemies and wild beasts will attack using the element of surprise. Your village trainers will prepare you to notice subtle clues of possible dangers and how to separate to effectively handle the issue, but such is for a future lesson. Right now, we hope to help you perform as one so when it is time to distance yourself from one another, you will still be able to sense your brothers' position and intent."

The boys worked all day learning to move as a group. Their trainers acted as attackers, pointing out strategies available to counter different occurrences. Anders even insisted on sharing some of the dirty practices other triads might employ to gain an advantage. After working with Hendrix and Johan for so many cycles, he had a vast knowledge of such tactics. He also had suggestions for handling such dishonorable actions.

By the second day, the boys were freed from the confinement of the rope. They moved like dancers across the patch of land where they trained. When one of them had to advance, the other two moved backwards to ensure no one could attack from behind.

But as the day wore on, the boys grew tired and hungry. Some of their focus waned. Loinbard tried to demonstrate how vulnerable Ulices was near the end of the day. He had advanced without signaling his brothers. The Konrad warrior moved in for the attack, meaning to prove how losing focus could be deadly. A hard, crushing blow from behind sent him falling to his knees. Turning around, he saw an arrogant Usman.

Jemina's loud gasp ripped down from the trees, but when the boy held out his hand to help Loinbard to his feet, she started chuckling with relief. "Sorry about that, sir," Usman smiled. "I hated to strike you, but my brother's protection was at risk. You did explain it was my duty to watch his back, right?"

16

Protecting the Fragile

Darnish stood on the platform at the center of the meeting area. The three groups of boys selected by the men to compete stood behind him. He told the children to go stand by their trainers to await further instruction. Finnegan dashed between the triads, tossing what appeared to be a sack toward them. Aras bent down to pick up the cloth and examine it.

"It's an egg apron," Jemina whispered. She stood far enough apart from them so it appeared she was listening to her father's words from the center.

True enough, the garment was lined with pockets from top to bottom and all the way around. Aras wondered at its importance as Loinbard offered words of encouragement to the boys they had worked with. "No matter what happens today, consider this your first chance to prove your worth to the elders. The win is not your primary focus."

Anders and Jemina scoffed at his comment. He stared back at them with resolve. "Have both of you forgotten the weight of competing in an official event for the first time? No one will claim the final, third victory of this challenge. Yet three future warriors will relive every mistake they chanced to make here today. Should we add the shame of costing their trainers a bit of glory on top of that?"

"Continue," Aras said, only half listening to what his blood brother said to the boys. They had discussed the importance of giving the children calming words to lead them into the event. Anders had been a part of the discussion, but he must have taken exception to the part about winning not being the focus.

"Work as a team. Be mindful of where your brothers stand and what dangers lurk around your whole triad. Communicate in ways only your mates can understand so you can keep the advantage of surprise," Loinbard concluded.

"Win this challenge," Jemina said just loud enough for the three youngsters to hear, "and I will put in a good word with the lead warrior fledglings train under."

The three boys smiled brightly at that promise and set their shoulders straight, awaiting orders from Darnish. The other groups were focused on the center platform as well. "Have the youngest of your group put on the egg apron. We will wait until this is done to continue."

Usman balked at the notion when Aras approached him. "I just outgrew this baby task," he protested. "Official fledglings never have to put that stupid thing on again."

Aras did not try to reason with the boy. Instead he gave Usher, the unspoken leader of the brothers a pointed expression. The teenage boy took a deep breath and accepted the responsibility of handling any strife within his group. "If Darnish, a seasoned warrior, instructs you to put on something, brother, you do it. One day we will be in his position. How would you feel if a new fledgling refused your command?"

The younger boy yanked the apron over his face crossly. "Fine, I will put it on, but if anyone laughs, I will punch them in the ball sack."

Darnish nodded with approval when his orders had been fulfilled. "The cooks want to prepare eggs for our morning meal following this challenge," he teased. "Send the boys in your charge to collect some from the henhouse."

"Is there a set number to be collected?" Tyler asked for his triad.

"We will allow each group to determine that for themselves," he replied, inclining his head in deferment. Aras noticed the other Konrad triad discussed matters with their children. He observed that the Finns' training mirrored their leader's arrogance. The older boys sent the youngest off to collect the eggs alone.

All the information he had surmised about Darnish's reasoning and his planning of this challenge rolled around in Aras' brain. He had an inkling of what was to follow and decided to follow his gut. "Usher, Ulices and Usman, listen carefully. Work to fill every single pocket of this apron with eggs. You older boys, concentrate on putting some in the places your brother cannot reach. Do not leave a single pocket empty. Do you two have pockets? Yes? Good, fill them with eggs, too. Don't leave a single egg behind if you can manage it."

"Do we steal the eggs of the other teams?" Ulices asked with cautious optimism. "Anders will be disappointed in such a dishonorable action, but if you think it is necessary…"

"No, do not take what is not yours. Once an egg is in the hand of another, it is off bounds," Aras said and chuckled when he noted the disappointment in Usman's tiny face at not being able to battle for the right to collect eggs. "Keep your chin up, young man." He laughed. "If I am correct, you will get to lay claim to the other teams' eggs soon enough."

Usman was a comical sight when he returned from the hens' house, his size nearly double due to the eggs he carried. The boy even had some in his arms, though he dropped a few as he tried to balance them and his wooden sword at the same time.

Hendrix and his group made no effort to hide their mocking comments. "It's a surprise someone with such short legs can walk, much less lug around his weight in eggs." Their own fledgling returned with his front pockets full, a resentful look on his face at being left to handle the demeaning task alone. One of his fellow team members pushed him down for daring to complain, breaking a few of the fragile shells in the apron. Johan cackled at the hint of yellow liquid slipping from the boy's egg sack material.

Tyler praised his group when they arrived back. Though a few pockets remained unfilled, a fair amount lined the child's apron. He and his triad gave a few words of praise to the boys they trained before turning back to the platform to await future instructions.

Laughing at the extra eggs the Konrad-Finn group had collected, Darnish offered a bit of advice. "You will need your hands and weapons for this task, young fledglings. Might I suggest you find a way to stow the surplus in your pockets?" He threw back his head to howl with appreciation a moment later. The boys had indicated to the already brimming compartments in their clothes.

Anders stepped forward to take advantage of the delay as Ellias, Leodon and Ellena shared humorous looks. The Finn warrior tied knots in the boys' shirts and pants, fashioning makeshift pockets. Then Aras and Loinbard help place the extra eggs in the new hiding places. They were careful to store the eggs in areas less likely to lead to accidental breakage.

Leodon saw their efforts and objected. "Your original rules only regarded the eggs carried in the apron, Darnish. Are you amending that now? This lot seeks ways to challenge our limits yet again. To allow for it would not be wise."

Darnish just smiled with delight. "You worry too much, my brother. How can anyone challenge rules, which have not even been laid out before them. I would not handicap any warrior who brings too many weapons to battle. Instead, I would watch how he manages to handle the excess until it is needed." He started to pace the length of the platform, carefully counting the number of steps back and forth, then to and from.

"If my calculations are correct, there is but ten square feet to maneuver up here. Three sets of grown warriors would have an issue moving about, but the young fledglings will have just enough room to do so. In a few minutes, the horn will sound. The triads will send their young charges up here. They will be given a brief moment to select a portion of the area to begin the quest. At the sound of the second horn, the game is on."

Stepping down, he moved among the young Urijah groups. "Be careful to stay on the platform, boys. Once you leave it, you will no longer be in the field of play and eliminated. So long as at least one of your group remains on top, your team is still part of the challenge."

"Are we meant to avoid breaking our eggs as we shove other boys off?" Usman asked politely.

"It is imperative to protect your own eggs, yes. In this task, they represent the weakest among you, depending on each of you to guard them, even if you get wounded in the process." Darnish explained, taking note of which child had been bright enough to ask.

"Sir, who would seek to harm our eggs? There are no evil-doers here. Who will play the role of enemy so we may show our skill?" The boy dared to question him again.

"You are one of Leodon's blood brothers' sons, right? Named Usman?" he looked back at Leodon for confirmation. A quick nod affirmed his guess. "Sometimes a foe is within your own village. It is sad, but true. You must not only defend yourself against outsiders, but protect what is yours from those around you, too. Do you understand my meaning now?"

The boy's face lifted with excitement. "We get to smash the other teams' eggs! Aras thought as much before you even mentioned the plan, sir. He is almost as wise and brave as a Urijah warrior."

Nodding with agreement, Darnish motioned to the triads. "Prepare your teams for the challenge. Know this. While you may provide advice when the game begins, only the young boys are allowed on the platform. Any triad breaking this rule will be eliminated from winning the task." A challenging glare was made in the direction of the Finn men. Crosby was confused and the others pretended to ignore the action.

Hendrix grabbed the two older boys in his charge the moment Darnish walked away. "Go after the boys wearing the apron. Don't waste time smashing stupid eggs. Pitch both from the playing field, and the win is ours."

Tyler and his group spoke to their group in a hushed tone. Aras bent low to do the same with his own team. "Usher, Ulices, you have spent years protecting Usman's back. Now you must rely on that skill to give us an added advantage in this quest. Do not concentrate on smashing any eggs unless you have a clear shot. Instead, stop anyone from breaking your brother's load. If one egg does get smashed, do not waste time regretting the loss. Instead, reach in your pockets and replace the broken egg with a new one."

Loinbard added his advice. "Do not be aggressive in your pursuit of the other egg bearers. Such an action might draw a counterattack. This is not a task that calls for a speedy victory. Lay low until the time is right and your group will benefit."

"But you promised I could smash some eggs!" Usman pouted, giving Aras a comical frown. He might have the wisdom and pride of an old soul, but his boyish demeanor shined through.

Anders carefully patted the boy's back, careful not to break any of the eggs. "That is the beauty of this task, little warrior.

You get to do what you know best. While your brothers must be careful and concentrate on protecting your back, you are free to move about the entire platform destroying as many eggs as possible. Trust they will be close by to block any blows aimed your way and have fun getting some of your blood thirsty tendencies out."

The horn signaled it was time for the boys to take their places. Aras lifted the smallest of their charges up and bid him luck. Usman walked to the middle of the platform, deciding it would be the best location to avoid getting eliminated. It also allowed him easy access to the rest of the area. He could dart in and out of the others, cracking as many eggs as possible before returning to the safety of mid-section.

"That boy will be an elder of Urijah one day," Aras told his triad.

"Without a doubt," Jemina said, no longer pretending she did not have a favorite in the challenge. She stood among the Konrad-Finn triad as if it were her rightful place. "All three of your charges are direct descendants of Urijah. Finnegan, Jael and me, too, if Grandpa Ian is to be trusted. They carry the bloodline of our first elder's DNA and are being groomed for accepting the duty of village leaders when the time comes."

The boys under the Finn Triad were quickly eliminated well before Crosby accidently tripped and landed on the platform. The other fledglings used that group's larger size and lack of teamwork to send Hendrix's chosen ones out of the field of play. The group trained by Tyler, Sage and Riley held their own, but they lacked the additional eggs to replenish lost ones. Once their last egg was cracked, they shook hands with the winners and stepped off of the platform. Usman pranced around the stage, pulling out his remaining eggs now that their last challengers were abolished. He turned his remaining stash into projectiles and hurled them at his brothers. Usher and Ulices used their wooden swords to bat the eggs back at him.

The entire area was soon covered in scrambled egg whites and yolks.

Aras lifted a slippery Usman to his shoulders while Anders and Loinbard did the same with the remaining brothers. They carried the victors off to where the morning meal was set to begin. "All hail Urijah!" The Konrad-Finn triad chanted, Jemina lending her high-pitched voice to the cheer.

17

Narrowing the field of competition

Tyler, Sage and Riley approached asking for a moment alone with Aras' triad. Jemina tried to join them, but was sent back to where her fathers and mother were finishing their meal. She started to argue when three hands lifted, ready to reply to any further defiance. Her eyes were back to being steel blue again as she stormed away.

"Congratulations on your win this morning," Sage said. "The elders of Konrad will be pleased to know our village not only produces worthy warriors, but excellent teachers as well."

"Had I not guessed about the advantage of having extra eggs, I am not so sure our team would have claimed this victory. You three would make fine trainers for the fledglings one day," Aras told the other triad. "Truth be known, your lot is the only real competition we worry about for Jemina's hand. The only way Crosby managed to claim one victory was because it literally fell in his lap."

"Then your third victory should be easy to accomplish," Tyler offered. "We are withdrawing from the competition after the meal is complete." He raised his hand to put off any arguments. "Our triad is set on taking this course. It is best to leave now while there may still be time to reclaim our position on the wall. Sometimes elders take up areas at the city left vulnerable on the off chance a winner will be declared quickly. The defeated triads can avoid losing a precious cycle of duty that way."

Riley shook hands with all three of the Konrad-Finn triad. "We might have provided you with more of a challenge in the coming events if it was not evident Jemina has already bonded with you three. She is a rare gift, and when you return to Konrad, we will celebrate in the treasure you earned. Until then, we return to our duty and prepare the way for your homecoming."

"We will leave the details of your triad's make up for you to share." Tyler smiled. "Explaining it would be too difficult. Besides, no one would believe us if we tried to explain how you three could come together from two different villages, perfect your team efforts and claim a village bride."

Later that night, Aras awoke to the sound of a dove's cry. He listened attentively for the number of coos, wondering if trouble was afoot. Stiffening with anticipation, he reached for his sword quietly. The call came again, and the others in his triad sat up, their weapons ready. Each counted the number sounded at four bustles and peered at one another with confusion. Was an actual dove in one of the trees a few feet away? They turned to search the area.

Abruptly Jemina's face popped out as the top of her body dropped into view. but her head was upside down. Their village bride was hanging from a branch by her knees, her lips pursed together in four, quick coos. All three men groaned in frustration.

"I claim the right to upend her this time," Aras grumped as he pulled himself up to head in her direction.

"This is her second transgression for the same offense. We each get a chance to impart our displeasure with her mistake," Anders announced as he and Loinbard followed suit.

"You already got a chance to enjoy feeling her backside

respond to your hand. I go second, and don't be surprised if I bare her ass before I take up the task." Loinbard heard the call of an eagle sound once. He turned toward the opposite direction.

Hands on his hips, he replied, "Yes, Grandfather Ian, I recall your presence. Your headstrong granddaughter needs to be tamed, sir. If she keeps showing up here at night, my brothers and I can't promise not to claim her. We trust you will slaughter us for the insult, but it is still tempting. Do not forget we love her and have pledged ourselves to her. Waiting to bed her is difficult enough without her pulling us off every chance she gets so we can share a stolen moment of privacy."

"Her ass remains covered until the ceremony, son of Konrad. I am not your grandfather yet." Not a hint of the older warrior was visible as he laid down the law. With a reluctant nod of agreement, Loinbard continued on to where Aras was now helping Jemina climb out of her hiding spot.

"Four coos- did you notice?" Jemina smiled with pride. "Given your clever calling system, I decided it was appropriate to claim my own signal. I wager no other family unit has secret ways of communicating without outsiders noticing."

"My fathers could convey many ideas within my family unit without opening their mouths," Anders muttered, with a dark expression marring his attractive features. "One pointed stare can say a lot about how someone is feeling. You might try to remember such a keen bit of insight and work on employing your skills on understanding unspoken messages. Do any of our faces suggest how we are feeling about your second act of defiance tonight?"

"Before any of you start lecturing me," she whispered bravely, "it is important for you to realize I have permission to be here this time."

Aras pulled her around to face him again. "Look me in the eyes, and tell me you did not sneak past your fathers to come here."

Jemina grabbed her backside even though no threats had been made on it as yet. "My mother and I decided it might be beneficial for me to come. She distracted my fathers to enable me to go outside without burdening them with needless worry."

Anders pulled her around to face him, making her dizzy. "Why would your mother betray her own mates for such a dangerous mission?"

Jemina found it hard to explain what had seemed so logical only a few moments before. "After the Konrad triad departed… because they saw how close we had become…" Her hand gestured toward the men and back to herself. "It's apparent how we all feel about each other. Mother and I wondered if maybe the other men will do the same as the Konrad triad did. Even if they lack honor, seeing a woman they hope to claim sneaking around at night with other men would have to be difficult to tolerate. We concluded the Finn warriors would leave in disgust at the humiliation, if nothing else."

Anders muttered a phrase any honorable warrior was careful to avoid expressing when women were about. Grabbing her arms, he gave Jemina a slight shake. "Creator above, give me patience!"

Loinbard turned her yet again, so he was inches from her face. "Your mother and you are naïve if you think Hendrix and Johan would willingly walk away from this competition. If they feel slighted by your actions, they won't withdraw. They have no honor. They are selfish enough to stay here and do their best to win your hand, brooding over your perceived slight. Then they would haul you off to their village to make you pay for embarrassing them. The rest of your life would be pure hell because you sought to outwit them."

"And you would have no one to appeal to for help." The last scolding came from her grandfather. He had remained hidden, but his voice indicated he was close at hand. "This has become intolerable, sons of Konrad and Finn. I give you leave to handle this indiscretion as you see fit. Just remember I am close enough to intervene if any of you try to take advantage."

Aras took Jemina by the hand and led her to a stump near the tree she had dropped from. The area was poorly lit, and it would afford them some privacy. It was important to protect her from view if anyone chanced by their location. "Will we be allowed to provide comfort afterwards? It is important to reset matters after any correction."

"Are all men of Konrad so bold, young man? Fine, you will have a few moments to share words of forgiveness and innocent kisses, but that is all!" The words were spoken in a tight tone. Jemina's eyes locked onto something off to the left. "Don't give me that defiant glare, Jemina, daughter of Urijah. I might well take a turn trying to pound some sense into your bottom."

Without giving her a chance to even acknowledge the threat, Aras took a seat and pulled her across his lap. His eyes examined what she wore. Their little spitfire had donned her fighter clothes to gain better camouflaging of her movements in the darkness.

Her careful consideration of dressing both pleased and concerned him. She was brilliant, a fierce warrior and beautiful soul. He paused a moment, then decided it was important to humble Jemina a bit since this was her second correction for the same rule. He reached under her and unfastened the clasp holding her pants in place.

She let out a shocked mewing sound as he tugged the clothing down and cool air touched her skin. Aras debated restoring the material as his eyes feasted on her perfect, pale ass. It was small and unblemished. He had to adjust his position as his cock grew uncomfortably thick. Protecting Jem was something he would never take lightly. She was his world now.

One hard palm smacked against her backside. His single handprint covered both globes, an angry mark appeared and he took care to use steady, measured strokes as he continued painting the rest of the region. She protested and started thrashing about so he used his left hand to anchor her as he began lecturing and spanking in unison.

"Think for a moment, my brilliant little fighter," he ordered. "What if we had not been the ones to find you tonight? Hendrix and Johan have no morals. They would assume you were offering yourself, and smuggle you off to enjoy the pleasure of using your body. If you did manage to explain you were not coming to see them but spend time with us, it would not matter. I fear they would only be more sadistic in their intent then.

"They would hold you down and take turns planting their seed in your womb. In their minds, your fathers would end the games and wed you to them before your humiliation could come to light." The more he spoke, the harder she struggled against him. His hand continued bouncing around her soft skin. It grew warm to the touch, but she still did not yield.

It was then he noticed the treasure exposed every time she kicked her legs in her attempts to escape. Red, plush folds guarded her secrets, and his cock grew so hard he had to alter his position yet again. The action paused his attention to her backside, and they both stilled. The Creator might strike him dead where he sat, but Aras could not deny himself. His hand slid down her backside, along the crease that separated the globes and to the treasure hidden between those folds.

She was wet and hot. His fingertip slipped just inside the opening he would rightfully claim one day. He groaned with desire and frustration. Pulling his hand away before his actions became more sinful. Aras helped Jemina back up and gained his own feet. He prayed his erection was not as evident as it seemed.

His palm, still hot from the attention he gave her backside lifted to cup her neck. He pulled her to him, his mouth parting as it sought hers. Jemina did not protest. Her lips melted against his and she gave his tongue leave to join with hers. He explored every crease, tasted every inch and sought to mark his claim with his scent.

Stepping away from her was difficult, but necessary. She was not his alone. It pained him, but in a society where men outnumbered women six to one, it was impossible to lay sole claim to one bride. One day, if the Creator saw fit, the disparity of such a number would be eliminated. His mind drifted for a moment to the city of women. Once revenge had been gained, many of the people inside might well leave the walls and join the different villages. Future generations, maybe even his own sons, would no longer have to share intimacies of a wife with other men.

Aras went to where his blood brother stood, relieving him to take his position with Jem.

LOINBARD FALTERED as he headed for her. Her back was to him and her glorious ass almost glowed in the moonlight. His body responded immediately. Walking was not easy with a hard rod straining against his pants. The Konrad warrior kept his eyes locked on her head; sure he would never recover if he allowed his focus to stray lower. Gaining the place where he would sit to correct her, he spoke in an even tone. "Do you need a moment to compose yourself before we continue?"

A defiant shake of the head was his only answer. "If you won't acknowledge the danger you put yourself in…"

"You three forget I am not some unskilled city bride. I have been trained in the art of protecting myself and those around me. The right to form a triad was not open to me, so I had to learn to become an extra to many groups of fighters, assessing their strengths and matching my performance accordingly. Hendrix and Johan would not find it easy to take advantage of me. It is insulting for any of you to suggest as much. I would gut them both before they even freed their cocks to spill their seed. Have you forgotten the first challenge so soon?"

Loinbard trained his eyes on her. "Deny your skill? Never. We take pride in it. The children our Creator blesses our future family unit with will be fierce warriors before they even become fledglings thanks to having a mother like you to prepare them. But even the best warriors fall victim of evildoers. Hendrix and Johan did not resort to the more brutal techniques they could use to gain every advantage available to them."

"I assure you, they fought hard to take away my sword." Her hands crossed under her chest with irritation. The pants she had been holding up now puddled around her ankles. Loinbard swallowed hard as he spied the patch of curly hair below her waist. It matched the shade of her head perfectly.

Returning his attention to her face, he did his best to focus. It took a strong shake of his head to clear his mind before he continued, "An audience, namely your fathers and two other triads of warriors were present. Fighting styles are more formal when others are around to take exception to unfair methods. Without others to intervene, men like them become unhinged. Anders has shared some tales of events he witnessed. Without him around to control their baser instincts, Hendrix and Johan would have slaughtered many innocent people in the quest for power."

Remaining quiet, he allowed his words to penetrate her thoughts. She was wise beyond measure. As a trained soldier, she would have learned to listen to correction from her trainers. Achieving the level of success she boasted, Jemina would be able to accept his wisdom once she comprehended the explanation. She finally gave him the briefest of nods.

Lifting his hand, he offered her help to carry out his next words. "Let's get this over with, Jem. Place yourself across my lap."

She stiffened and was back to being defiant. "Can't you just position me yourself, like Aras did, and Anders the occasion before?"

"You are not a child below us, village bride. When we are

wed, you will be an equal member of our family. As such, you have a voice in all our decisions. It also means you accept responsibility for poor choices which go against the group consensus. By placing yourself over my knees, you are accepting the loving guidance we offer and promising to learn from the experience." His hand still remained raised, waiting for her to take it when she was ready.

Jemina's usual agile movements were hampered by the pants around her ankles and the resentment of following through with the command. Time passed slowly, but she found her way to his side and awkwardly placed herself across his solid legs. "You please me," Loinbard told her, his hand running gently across her already punished skin. "Your trust and bravery have changed my mind about the initial fifty strokes I planned to administer."

Raising up on her hands, she glared back up at him. "Fifty!"

"It is your second warning about sneaking out at night." He did his best not to grin at her expression. "I think half that number will get my point across. The first twenty will bring some of the heat back to the portion my blood brother already covered. The last five will be against the top of your perfect thighs. That area is more sensitive and will hold the sting longer, helping you recall the disadvantage of requiring a repeated correction."

"One question before you begin," she said. He almost ignored it, thinking she was trying to put off the evitable, but honored the request. "Had Hendrix and Johan managed to attack me, what would the triad of Konrad and Finn have done?"

"Before or after we slit their throats?" he asked without pause.

Instead of qualifying her question, Jemina gave him a slight nod of acceptance and lowered herself again. She flinched as he set about counting the first twenty, but he sensed she was fighting against the urge to pull free. Seeing the delightful way her ass responded with a slight bounce with each impact of his hand, Loinbard told himself he should be ashamed of the desire raging inside him. But he wasn't. Everything about Jemina felt right, from the establishment of a group of husbands bonded for the sole purpose of claiming her, to the treasure of holding her this close, she was meant to be theirs.

18

Ellias' Challenge

Konrad-Finn Triad: 2 wins

Finn Triad 1: win

Anders grew weary of waiting his turn. The soft moans tearing from Jemina's throat were wreaking havoc on his body. Part of him wanted to step in and end the pain she endured. Yet he would never forgive himself if she repeated this defiance because of his leniency. If anything happened to her, it would be his fault for not doing his duty by her.

Something was hurled from the darkness of the tree line. The Finn warrior's fast reaction was the only thing preventing the item from smacking him between the eyes. Aras raised a shoulder seeking to know what was going on. Anders lifted the object in his hand to show him and they both glanced back at the direction it came from. One hand was lifted in the air, the rest of Grandfather Ian's body hidden. Anders inclined his chin to signal his understanding. The decision of whether or not to forgo his part of the punishment had been decided without his input.

The sound of hand against flesh had ceased for many moments and Anders tired of waiting patiently for Loinbard to relinquish his time with Jemina. Turning his head, he found his new brother embracing her, their mouths locked together. The kiss was not what rankled his nerves. It was the liberty the younger man was taking despite having Urijah soldiers close by. He sent his signal that hardly resembled a dove's peaceful call as it should. Loinbard's hand reluctantly moved away from Jemina's small breast and settled on her tiny waist. He lingered with the kiss a bit longer, though.

Finally allowed to leave his position protecting her privacy, Anders steeled his resolve. Still dazed from Loinbard's passionate attention, it took her awhile to notice what he held in his hand. Jemina took a step away, nearly toppling over the stump her first two mates had used. Anders caught her before any harm would befall her and pulled her upright carefully.

"Yours?" she asked in a husky voice.

"No, but I will likely require one like it after our wedding if tonight's activities are any indication." He folded the leather strap in half and gave her the intended number to follow. "Five across your sit spot, Jem."

She did not look pleased, but spared them both any futile protest. "Will you force me to place myself over your lap this time?" Her voice was weak, but her determination was steady. Their brave bride was submitting to them. Their bond was as solid as any merged family unit he had known.

"You won't be laying across my lap. Face the stump and bend over. Use your hands to brace yourself if needed. I do not want you to fall over and harm yourself." She mocked his choice of words with a raised brow. Jemina moved sluggishly, but she obeyed his orders. The hard wood provided her with something to balance against.

Her head turned back. It was flush from her embarrassing position. "One more question, Anders, if you please."

It was hard not to grin at her sass. Her pride might be wounded, but it would recover and they would quickly get past this slight disruption to their growing connection. "Ask anything of us, Jemina."

She glanced another look back at him and smiled. "Thank you for the offer. I shall ask a couple then." Anders bit the inside of his cheek to help him maintain a stern expression. "First, do I get to take a leather strap to your backside if you disrespect a rule I set in place for your own good?"

A hooting of amusement coming from the direction where Grandfather Ian concealed himself sent Anders' teeth grinding. Even the fellow members of his triad could not hide their response. "All rules set forth by our family unit will be agreed on by the majority. Yes, there will be times when I do not make good choices and will face the consequences. Aras and Loinbard will take great pleasure in knocking me on my ass to clear any hard feelings. But in truth, I fear your methods of extracting punishment when you are our wife. You have a keen mind and long memory. A leather strap would be a fleeting chance to demonstrate your displeasure so I doubt you will employ it. Your next question, Jem?"

"Let us consider the unlikely chance I would be bested by such disreputable men as Hendrix and Johan. After you three avenge my fate, what happens then? How would the three of you proceed after that point, when I might be carrying another triad's child?"

All sounds of amusement abruptly ceased. Anders walked to stand beside her, bending down so their faces were inches apart. "Any child which comes from your womb would be a proud, worthy descendent of Urijah. It pains me to admit it, but Hendrix and Johan share the same ancestral genes as I do. Your babe would be a credit to the Finn Village. Finally, your child becomes our child and will be raised in the Konrad Village, learning all its rich customs and honored traditions. The only shame our triad would bear is knowing we failed to protect you in a time of need. We would double our efforts to never let you or the child you bless our family unit with down again."

She stood up and took a moment to allow the earth to stop spinning. Then Jemina threw herself into his arms. Her mouth reached up for his. Anders needed no further urging. He pulled her tightly to his chest and sealed his promise with a deep kiss. An eagle's call ended the passionate exchange and he reluctantly let her slide down his length so she could regain her footing.

Her eyes locked on the section of his groin, which strained against his pants. He sucked in his breath when she reached out her small hand. He was sure she meant to touch his throbbing cock, but she grasped his right hand instead. The left, his dominant still held the belt. Jemina lifted his palm and brought it to rest on the gentle slope of her breast.

Her heart pounded wildly against it. She gave him a few seconds to enjoy her wild response to his touch before pulling the palm up to place a sweet kiss. Smokey blue eyes darted up and she bared her teeth playfully. She bit down on the fleshy area before smoothing the affected area with her tongue. Dropping his hand, she stepped out of the pants around her ankles and returned to the position he had ordered her to assume before.

His own legs were not steady as he stood off to the side. Clutching the belt tightly, he arched his hand back and applied the first stripe across the most sensitive part of her bottom. Another followed, slightly above, then another below. He did not put much force behind the strokes, but her pale skin still showed the damage of leather against flesh.

The last two were the hardest for him to deliver. Jemina had recoiled after every application of the belt. She bravely forced her body to provide him with a clear target. Anders applied the last two strikes in a crisscrossing pattern, connecting all the welts.

It would be a long time before their Jem would forget this correction. Every time she sat; the discomfort would be a constant reminder of what would follow if she put herself in harm's way again.

AS FAR AS the competition went, Jemina's family considered her as good as claimed by the Konrad-Finn triad. But tradition maintained the challenges continue until one group had rightfully collected three wins. This weighed heavily on Ellias as he sought to develop a fair task, which might still provide Aras, Anders and Loinbard with an advantage.

He had spent some time with the triad from Konrad before they departed. He gathered much from the young men. They felt Aras' group was vastly more prepared to travel between the villages without coming to great harm. The game should involve traversing the territory out of their village. Ellias had thought to seek his wife's advice on the challenge he decided on to get her insight.

Unfortunately, Ellena was not talking to any of her mates at the moment. Ian, one of the youngest Urijah elders and Leodon's father, had paid their family unit an unannounced visit last night. Jemina had taken a nightly stroll, and their dear wife had helped their daughter sneak away.

There was no question. The husbands had to sanction Ellena. She held her position as each applied a cane to her backside. They assumed this signaled her understanding of the need for punishment for the disgraceful action. Yet she held herself stiff when they tried to comfort her afterwards. Sometimes he questioned if they were too lenient in their discipline. If she continued to pout much longer, Ellias would suggest another session with the cane to see if her disposition improved any.

"After the wedding ceremony, our daughter's new mates will

be taking her away from the protection of our village. It pains us to have her far away, but it would help ease our minds if we could be assured, she will be well cared for no matter where she goes. The challenge I offer is this. Tonight, both triads will spend the night outside our village boundaries, with only your weapons and wits to protect your backs.

"Return at dawn, bringing with you any proof of the dangers you managed to eliminate, so we can understand your survival skills." Ellias waited for any questions. He hoped he would be able to provide an adequate answer. He wanted these games over and done with. Ellias did not trust the Finn warriors and every moment they occupied Urijah land worried him more. How imprudent he and his triad had been to allow such evil men the honor of trying to win Jemina's hand.

She had seemed so taken with Crosby during her time with him. He lacked true intelligence and they planned to reject him outright if he appeared at the border. But Hendrix and Johan had hidden their true manner when they arrived, Crosby in tow. Ellias had foolishly thought the older, more seasoned warriors would make up for the witless one. Jemina would have a man she desired and two others capable of protecting her he had falsely reasoned.

He would personally see these two dead before allowing them to wed her now. Hoping not to chance starting a war with their allies, the Finn village, he purposely kept secret the details of what the triads should collect to claim victory in this challenge. Ellias and his triad would give the win to Konrad-Finn no matter what either team returned with the next morning.

When the sun rose over the horizon, most people present wanted to spill the Finn men's blood after they returned with a trophy, arrogantly secure that victory was theirs.

JEMINA BARELY NOTICED Aras was cradling something in his strong arms as the Konrad-Finn triad returned. Her eyes rushed from one to the other, searching for any signs of trouble they may have had to contend with during their night outside the protection of the village. She smiled brightly when no noticeable wounds could be found. Aside from Aras, their hands were empty. Had they returned with nothing to prove their skill to Ellias?

She took heart for the moment; there was still no sign of the other triad. Jemina felt ashamed of her pleasure about their absence. The Creator had to understand her secret desire that something would stop the Finn triad from being able to return to Urijah. She did not wish them death, only some humbling experience that sent them back to their own homes and far from her.

The Konrad-Finn triad followed tradition, greeting her fathers and mother before seeking Jemina out. A pitiful hissing sound escaped from whatever Aras carried. He lifted a scrawny bundle of fur to his face and made soothing sounds by the creature's ears. Shrieking with thrill, Jemina rushed to examine the treasure.

"What is it?" she asked, prying the soft animal from his hold. "Why does it look so sickly?"

Aras stroked the animal's head. "It's a cub, maybe a cougar, but I cannot be sure. It's bellows of hunger prevented us from gaining a moment's sleep until we sought it out. Loinbard and Anders cleared the immediate area, making sure no mother cat would show up and attack us for touching her baby. I pulled this little fellow from a small cave just south of here."

Anders and Loinbard moved closer until the four of them formed an intimate circle. The Finn warrior scratched behind the cub's ears. "The mother must have been killed, leaving this little creature orphaned."

Loinbard extracted a bit of meat from his pocket and broke off a small piece to feed the cat. "Its mother must have perished a long time ago. The cat was close to death by the time Aras extracted him from his hiding place. We've been taking turns feeding him through the night. He's a survivor. Aras thought your healer may offer suggestions to care for him until we can release him back into the wild."

"Konfin Kitty may not want to be released," Jemina announced.

"Konfin Kitty?" Aras mocked. "I think our little Jem has not only decided to lay claim to this scrappy bit of fluff, but she's already named it in our honor. Sneaky move, Jemina. Are you trying to turn our pride against us by using our village names?"

"He doesn't look like a Smiley, and the worthy warriors of Konrad and Finn did rescue him," she said, her eyes sparkling with joy.

A snide voice tore Jemina's attention away from the animal purring in her arms. "Is that pitiful creature all the Konrad-Finn warriors have to show for their night outside the village limits?" Johan smirked. "Did you bring some cute little bunnies, too?"

HENDRIX STROLLED ACROSS THE BORDER; a sack laid carelessly over one shoulder. Crosby appeared next, a look of despair etched across his face. The attractive Finn warrior quickly found his way toward Jemina's parents.

"I had no part in this," he told them. "I tried to prevent it from happening, but they would not heed my protest. I cast off both men as members of my triad. I would rather return to my village to spend the rest of my days alone, than spend another moment in their company."

Aras reached to pull Jemina behind his back. Everyone was tense as all eyes regarded Hendrix cautiously. What was concealed within the sack? Not a harmless cub, for sure. Darnish brushed past Crosby to assume a defensive position near the Finn soldier in case it was necessary. Leodon and Ellias wisely placed their wife between them, ready to protect her if needed. They trusted Jemina was safely guarded by the warriors who would soon call her wife.

Unaware of the turmoil they were causing, Hendrix rushed to explain what the other triad had brought back with them. Johan sneered in Aras' direction. "Is that how Konrad warriors show their might? Bringing animals for their hosts to be burdened with caring for?"

He roughly lifted the sack from his shoulder and tossed it carelessly to the ground at the Konrad-Finn triad's feet. A groan of agony escaped the satchel, and the women present gasped in dismay. "While you were off playing with kittens, we used our time away from the village to eliminate real threats to our future in-law's home."

Johan dared to smile at Ellena when he spoke. "There is one less evildoer lurking close to your home, madame." He turned and hauled back his leg to strike the sack when Jemina's dagger impaled his thigh. Bellowing in outrage, he pulled it out and stepped toward her. Her three, overprotective grooms formed a wall around her, daring him to move closer.

"Slowly step away from the sack," Ellias ordered Hendrix and Johan. With a snap of his fingers, Jemina's eldest father called up dozens of warriors to defend them. Fierce, armed men appeared from behind bushes, trees, buildings and ditches to flood the area. The Finn men were relieved of their weapons and soon bound with their hands behind them. Only Crosby remained liberated, having wisely distanced himself from the horrible acts of his former triad.

The threat eliminated, Loinbard stepped toward the sack and carefully pulled it open. A small boy lay motionless inside. He could not be more than five or six cycles old, but someone had maliciously beaten him from head to toe. Rage consumed the older man, and he rushed toward Hendrix with his sword drawn.

Leodon intercepted him, reminding him justice would be served, but now was not the time.

Ellena wailed with dismay at the deplorable sight, but Jemina did not allow herself that luxury. She rushed to help the boy laying prostrate on the ground. Her hand moved to his swollen neck to search for signs of life. There was not an inch of skin unmarred by cuts or bruises on his small body. She refused to give in to the nausea welling in her throat.

"Quickly, someone help me get this child to Dalia. He is still alive, but only just." The village bride removed the delicate cape she had worn to help protect her from the morning breeze. It had been a treasured gift from Grandfather Ian. Jemina carefully used it to slow down the flow of blood on his chest.

Aras gently lifted the boy, recognizing him as the youngest of the two small children they saw the day their triad had been born. The innocent child had been appalled when his brother had killed a dove to feed their family. He was too young to comprehend harming a peaceful creature. That innocence had been stolen from him.

Two different emotions thundered through Aras now: remorse at not being able to stop this travesty from ever taking place and hatred toward the evil men who boasted of this cowardly act. The boy needed to be taken care of first; Aras ordered himself to walk away from exacting revenge. Loinbard rushed ahead to warn the healer what she would soon be dealing with. Anders shadowed behind Jemina, ready to catch her in his strong arms if necessary. Aras only hoped others would not kill the Finn evildoers before he could return to claim the honor.

19

The Claiming

The Joining Ceremony began after the boy was no longer close to death. Alistrair, the lead elder, presided and blessed the marriage after the triad repeated their oaths of protection and honor. Aras and Loinbard wore their finest Konrad colors and Anders showed off his Finn shades. Jemina, wearing the first-generation dress of her ancestors stood before each man, promising to love, honor and protect them also. No one noticed the slight rip where Smiley's sharp teeth latched on during the second challenge.

"Sir, I find it strange we have not seen you since the first night of our arrival." Later Aras accepted Alistrair's blessings as they walked toward a great feast prepared for the union. "From the way Jemina spoke of you, I half expected you to be a more active member of the challenges."

"From the moment three outside triads crossed our border, I have been within eyesight of every aspect of the competition. The elders and I carefully watched each set of men, deciding who would watch over whom until the winner was declared. My dear friend, Ian saw the way Jemina reacted to your triad. He insisted his own triad take responsibility for guarding you."

"Jemina did not care for me at first. I offended her, and it put me at a disadvantage from the beginning," the Konrad warrior explained. "I am not surprised Grandfather Ian wanted to protect her from me."

Alistrair managed a chuckle, despite his solemn demeanor. "He sought to defend you from her, and his fear that I grant her too much control over her future. Ian knew she was determined from the very start to wed your triad. He wanted to make sure you earned the right, and I did not interfere in the outcome."

"Did the guards report to you on the various things they witnessed?" he pressed the elder.

"We all gathered at different occasions to pass on critical information. Unfortunately, I spent most of my time shadowing the one called Johan. An unholy source resides in that man's heart, if he even has such an organ. I dared not sleep for fear of the harm he might cause. When the triads left the village border for the last challenge, I made a critical miscalculation. It will haunt me for the rest of my days. I told the guards to stand down and get some much-needed sleep while the outsiders were away. Had I not given into the temptation of rest; I might have been able to prevent the injustice inflicted on that innocent child."

THE PLACE of the first claiming brought about several challenges. Dalia was still caring for the small boy on the ground level healer's compound. Tradition held that new family units shared their first time as husbands and wife in this area. Grooms' joined their blood to introduce to the doors sealing each level of a new line. Aras and Loinbard were aware of secret threats hidden within the inner most circle. Entering such a foul place went against every fighter's instinct they knew.

"Is there another place we can spend the night?" Aras asked.

The question confused Jemina, who was yet unaware of their

tragic history. All of her life, she had seen new family units follow the binding ritual by going into the healer's building. There had never been any question in her mind that she would follow the same path. "The first level has been adjusted," she told her new husbands when the Konrad warriors hesitated at the door. "A protective wall was activated, portioning off the area where the boy rests. Dalia will have complete privacy as she watches over him. They will not be able to see or hear us."

"Are you concerned about our bride's privacy?" Anders was just as perplexed.

"Jemina," Loinbard took her into his arms. "Is your heart set on this location to begin our claiming?"

"All married units from our village begin their lives here. Each section is marked by our blood unit so when the time comes to welcome our children, the last seal may be broken for their birth." She was anxious enough worrying about the coming coupling. After all they had gone through, why was there hesitation now? Didn't her new husbands want to bed her?

"Our children will be born in Konrad." Aras worked hard to keep his tone even, void of all emotion. "Any blood bonds will be recognized there."

"Our children will be descendants of Urijah, Konrad and Finn. Creator forbid any of us perish, but it is important for our children to be assured a welcoming home in all three places. Am I mistaken?" Her voice cracked with sentiment.

Pulling her close to him, Aras realized he could no longer make decisions solely on his personal feelings. His devotion to Jemina was more important than maintaining his vow to shun everything connected with the building. His bride was still unaware of the secret he harbored, as was Anders. He would not burden them with it until they reached Konrad land. "You are our center force. If this is where you feel comfortable for the first claiming, so be it."

He bent down to a knee. Aras slowly eased the material of

her dress upward, uncovering smooth, pale skin. He stopped when the jeweled handle of a dagger tied at her thigh appeared. With great care, the Konrad warrior extracted the weapon before carelessly tossing it to Anders. His fingers returned to Jemina's smooth, silky skin. He could not stop himself from teasing her inner thigh with his lips, making her gasp. His own soft groans warned Aras it was best to get their bride inside before continuing.

Taking her dagger back from Anders, Aras placed it in Jemina's grasp. "This is a relic from Urijah, if I am not mistaken."

She nodded. "Grandfather Ian gave it to me after the joining ceremony."

"Mark me with it, bride," he demanded. When she hesitated, Aras guided the hand she cupped the knife with. The sharp edge sliced upon the palm of his hand. Blood soon welled up and he smiled. Parting the top of her dress with his unwounded hand, he exposed her perfect breasts. Aras planted the bleeding palm over her chest. Returning to his knee again he gave his pledge.

"Jemina, village bride of Urijah, chosen bride of Konrad-Finn, I claim you as my one true mate. I will protect you from head-on attacks, sacrificing my blood if needed to save yours." He stayed on his knees, but extracted his own knife from his side. He passed it to Anders. "Have her use it to draw your blood."

Anders had to help Jemina complete the task. Soon his blood stained the Konrad weapon. Walking first to her left, then to her right, he placed his palm on her arms before taking a knee. "I claim you, beautiful Jemina, as my mate. I will protect you from lateral attacks, sacrificing my blood if needed to save yours." Already understanding what Aras had intended, Anders removed his own Finn dagger and gave it to Loinbard.

He cautiously tossed it to Jemina, who caught it with the reflexes of a skilled warrior. Loinbard extended his palm with a smile. I believe you are meant to use the Finn weapon to complete our symbolic joining of villages, bride. Do you need assistance?"

A full smile crossed Jemina's face and she playfully shook her head. Making the barest of slices across his palm, she flinched when he cried out in pain. Loinbard's playful wink mocked her innocence. She squeezed the wound to elicit more blood and chuckled when he really did cringe a bit. He used his good palm to give her a disapproving smack on the ass before marking her back.

"Jemina, sassy female warrior of Urijah, chosen bride of Konrad-Finn, I claim you as my one true mate. I will protect you from surprise attacks, sacrificing my blood if needed to save yours."

Those words marked the official final pledge of their union. But this was no ordinary family union. Jemina held up her own palm and used all three knives to prick her own skin. She bent down, marking her husbands' foreheads. "Aras, Anders, Loinbard, I claim you three as my only true mates. I will protect you and all children raised by our family unit."

A huge bedframe dominated the ground level of the healer's compound when they entered. The four of them stared at it for a moment, knowing everything from the past had led to this path. "Well, husbands, I trust the cast-offs who trained you in the art of pleasing a wife prepared you for this moment. My inexperience concerns me, to be honest; I only hope I do not disappoint any of you."

Aras removed all the weapons he carried, both openly and in concealed places. He carefully placed them close at hand in case the need to use them presented itself. "I cannot speak for Anders, but Loinbard and I share your apprehension, bride. We never sought the services of the Konrad cast-off women. They are controlled by a spiteful female who spreads strife whenever possible."

Anders eyes widened. "You are both virgins?"

"I prefer the term celibate," Loinbard protested.

Aras sought to clarify their status. "The use of other women to train men for a future bride is not always productive. No two women enjoy the exact same things. My second mother lectured all of her sons on as much every chance she could. Seeking physical pleasure was not sinful in itself, but pretending to do so for false reasons was unfair to all involved."

Jemina rewarded both of the Konrad warriors with deep kisses. "We shall learn what pleases each other together," she said.

"Wonderful," Anders muttered. "Instead of our bride being the only inexperienced one among us, I get to be the filthy bastard who spent cycles seeking help to master all the different ways to make a woman scream with pleasure."

"There is more than one way?" Jemina asked with a wicked smile. "You must teach us every single method."

Chuckling with relief that she was not disappointed in him, Anders agreed to the task. "Women should never be rushed. Every action is a chance to prove how lucky a mate feels to be claiming her attention. Undressing is a good beginning point." With a quick glance at Aras and Loinbard, he asked, "Shall we begin to unwrap this wonderful wife we have earned?"

ARAS and his blood brother helped Jemina maintain her balance while Anders gently cupped first her right calf, then her left, to remove her shoes. Tossing them aside, he stood up to gather her long hair in his hands so one of the others could unfasten the buttons at the rear of her dress. Her head bent slightly, and she watched tan hands ease the garment down her shoulders. Hands at her sides, she did not even bother to attempt halting the material's descent as it puddled at her ankles.

Her husbands started circling around her, taking in her

nearly naked form, discovering the last secrets of her privacy. The murmured words of praise and lust. So sweet was the sound, Jemina found herself growing damp. Every nerve ending across her body was alert and ready for them to stroke.

"Ease your undergarment off, bride," Aras demanded.

Trembling fingers grasped the ties of cloth covering her most intimate parts. When the material gave way, she could not stop her hands from reaching down to shield the area. Loinbard clicked his tongue at her with reproach. "How can we study our gift if you hide it from view?" Her hands slowly inched away, and he rewarded her with a huge smile.

"When do I get to unwrap my presents?" she tried to sound confident but failed.

Anders and Loinbard continued circling her, but Aras stopped to stand before her. He lifted her hands in his own and kissed the palms. Then he placed them on the front of his shirt and invited her to remove his clothing. With shaking fingers, it took a bit of time, but she managed to do away with the garment. She smiled both with pride in her our accomplishment, and pleasure at seeing his toned stomach and solid arms.

His eyes met hers with a challenge, then lowered to his pants. Aras did not guide her hands to the buttons, giving her as much time as needed to find the courage. Jemina's chest responded to her increased heart rate by rising and falling wildly; she unfastened the buttons and used her hands to guide the cloth over his lean hips. It gave her something to do besides glare at the thick, long rod straining upwards.

Aras bent to reward her efforts with a deep kiss. Reluctantly he stepped back and began circling her. Anders presented himself next. She giggled nervously before removing his shirt and pants. His engorged member sprung outward. She moaned from surprise and appreciation. The Finn warrior pulled her to him and captured her mouth with determination. Only after his tongue had swept across every bit of her sweet mouth did he set her free. He was back to circling again, repeating his pledge to protect and care for her for the rest of their days.

Loinbard greeted her with a wide smile. Many of the buttons on his clothes had already been undone. A wicked grin suggested he was tired of waiting. Gulping hard, Jemina pulled off his shirt, her fingers lingering over the firm, hot skin of his chest. His hips were hard as rock as she freed him from his pants. Yet another heavy erection pointed at her. Lifting her high into his arms, he kissed her until the look of fear was replaced with passion.

Somehow, she had ended up in the center of the bed, Anders at her right and Loinbard at her left. Aras stood at the foot of the bed. As leader of their family unit, he had the first right to bury himself deep inside her. Jemina's eyes locked on his huge shaft and wondered if it might tear her.

Aras made no move to stake his claim. Instead he watched as Anders and Loinbard began exploring her breasts, neck and mouth. Fingers stroked slowly at first, then with an increased desire. She felt someone take the tip of one breast into a hot mouth and suckle. Another nipped at her neck. Jemina did not realize her legs had been parted at first. Hands gently inched her knees up before adjusting them so her core was open and ready to explore.

Fingers skimmed along her inner thighs, across her swollen folds and over a sensitive bud. Lifting her head, Jemina tried to distinguish which of her husbands was being so bold. She found three different hands moving around her most private region. Aras spoke and his words made her stiffen.

"Shall we all see how tight our bride is?" His finger poised at the opening of her core. Two others soon joined it there. On his word, they softly began pushing inside her. Jemina began to tense with fear even though they were not hurting her.

Aras took her hand and placed it over her swollen clit. "Touch yourself, bride. Show us how to please you."

Four different hands worked to prepare her body for claiming. Jemina watched her mates' lustful expressions as they worked to gently knead her channel wider. Her fingers danced across her clit, and she grew damper and more excited with each passing moment. "I do not know if I can withstand much more of this delicious torture, husbands."

Aras climbed between her legs the moment his brothers' fingers were removed. He guided the tip of his cock inside and waited for Jemina to signal her consent for him to continue. But she had continued rubbing herself and was now past noticing anything but the delightful waves of pleasure pulsing through her body.

He wanted to be patient, to wait until he was sure she was ready for him, but her expression of glory was too much to handle. Aras surged forward, only stopping when he was completely submerged inside her heat. Then his body's own instincts took over. He was pumping inside her. He spilled his seed much faster than he would have liked. Anders pushed him aside when Aras could not find the strength to concede his place.

Since it was only the first claiming, the Finn warrior did not intend to penetrate his bride with his cock, only gift her with his seed as he stroked himself to completion. Jemina reached up to touch him. She spread her legs wider and urged him to bury himself inside. He should wait, he knew. It was the honorable thing to do.

Anders sank inside and did not even find the willpower to hold back his release until he could move in and out a few times. His body jerked over hers as his hot seed poured deep within her womb. He muttered words of praise as he eased off of her, followed by regret for not waiting for the second night to claim her.

Jemina pushed aside the last remarks before motioning for Loinbard to come to her. "I am not a city bride to be eased into the process of claiming. I am a village daughter, ready to carry all my husbands' seed and know their love for me."

Loinbard pulled her knees to wrap around his waist. "Eyes open, bride. I want to see your expression when we join together."

Bits and pieces of past dreams popped into her mind, but Jemina pushed them aside for the present. Eyes wide, she stared at her third mate as he slowly positioned himself at her entrance. "Jemina, village daughter of Urijah, bride of Konrad and Finn, you make us complete."

20

Truth and Justice for All

Several elders and warriors from the Village of Finn arrived before sunrise the next day. They listened quietly to the charges brought against Hendrix and Johan by Alistrair, the leader and Urijah ruler. Jemina had never seen the elder so enraged.

He paced with bitter energy as he spoke. "Only by the grace of the Creator above did those two not succeed in their efforts to murder a child just past suckling age." He pointed where Hendrix and Johan sat just behind their own village leaders. "Our healer wept as she used a needle to sew up the more serious of wounds in hopes of stopping the blood loss. The damage inflicted on his tiny body was so extensive: he lay still as death the entire time. I watched as Dalia worked. The boy did not even flinch once."

Enoch, the head Finn elder maintained an emotionless stance, but many of the others who had traveled with him could not. One Finn warrior could not hold back his disgust and spat at the men being tried. Further reaction was blocked when Enoch stood to raise his hand. "Until judgment is passed, no one will seek to deliver punishment. We are a civilized people and will act as such."

He walked toward Alistrair, mindful to show respect as he waited to be acknowledged. "Your words suggested the boy survived. What arrangements have been made for his future care? The villagers of Finn stand ready to claim him as one of their own. No further harm will come to him. You have my word on it."

Aras gained his feet. "The child has already been claimed, sir."

Enoch turned to regard the warrior who dared to speak without being recognized by an elder. His disdain increased when he noticed the Konrad colors Aras wore. "Why is an outsider privy to this private matter? Only descendants of Urijah and Finn are involved."

Jemina immediately popped up and rushed to stand beside her groom. She had to fight her way through a small crowd, though. In the short time it took her to react, Anders, Loinbard, her parents, brothers and various Urijah warriors showed their support by surrounding Aras. She heard Grandfather Ian offer to respond to Enoch's inquiry.

"Aras is not only a son of Konrad, but he has a triad bond with a descendent of your own leader, Finn. More significantly, he is the lead husband of Urijah's own village bride." With a curt nod, he gave one final qualifier. "I am proud to claim him as grandson."

Loinbard gave his brother a playful punch before shaking Aras' hand. Turning to where Elder Ian stood, he called out. "Glad to know you finally admit to claiming us, Grandfather Ian," he teased.

"Who says I claim you? You are the last of the three grooms. Do not call me grandfather again until after the third claiming. For all I know, Jemina may decide she is happy enough with Anders and Aras and doesn't need you."

Snuggling between all three of her future mates, Jemina smiled at her grandparent's teasing. "Loinbard knows I love him just as much as I do my first two husbands. As for the second and third claiming, all were accomplished last night. All three are my true mates now, Grandfather Ian."

She boldly asked Alistrair if he would allow her to speak to the Finn Elder. Urijah's elder released some of the tension racking through his body. He always did have a soft spot for her and waved her forward. Jemina performed a perfect curtsey to Enoch, surprising him. Villagers rarely showed such respect for leaders of other areas, worried it might signal a wavering of allegiance.

"Hello, sir. It is an honor to meet you again." She smiled at him, and his demeanor calmed.

"I remember you well, Jemina, village daughter of Urijah. The birth of a girl in the villages is rare, indeed. Having the pleasure of traveling with one is unheard of. I am not surprised so many of our warriors asked to be relieved of their duties so they might travel here and seek your hand."

"My fathers allowed four of the men from your village to compete, sir. I was humbled by their interest. The men in Finn are impressive fighters, indeed. Your founding father Finn must have been an attractive man. Maybe Crosby resembles him? You no doubt recall how fascinated I was with Crosby when you graciously allowed us to join you and his triad on the way to the city." Jemina blushed at the memory. How could she have ever been so shallow she wondered?

Enoch moved closer, not wanting others to hear the admission he was about to make. "Women do seem inclined to gaze upon Crosby. His mother is quite proud of his appearance and the attention it affords her. She has spent considerable time and effort in shielding him from all activities that might disfigure her prize possession. I had hoped time with his original triad, away from her interference, would give him a chance to grow."

"My fathers saw his potential, too," she exaggerated, and heard a warning coo from Aras, and decided it was best to stick to the facts. "In truth, they allowed Crosby in because they thought to please me. Had they had more time to take Hendrix and Johan's measure, they probably would have excluded the triad completely."

"I am still reeling from the shock of those two casting Anders aside. I had worked hard to give them the best warrior of their training cycle. Had it not been for his leadership, Hendrix and Johan would never have progressed enough to guard the wall." Again, he offered the information in hushed tones.

Jemina did not lower her own. "The Village of Finn must be proud of its son, Anders. He is an honorable man, skilled warrior and handsome male. It may be fanciful to admit as much, but I believe the Creator intended for me to marry him because Anders is the perfect mate for me."

"Yet you are wed to men from Konrad?" Enoch mocked gently.

"Aras and Loinbard are excellent balances to Anders' skills. While within our village border, all three have worked as a team to win challenges, represent their villages with pride, and protect me from harm." She did whisper the next part. "From Hendrix and Johan when necessary, and my own foolish actions on occasion."

Enoch threw back his head and laughed. "Am I mistaken, or did the Urijah Village bride claim her husbands instead of the other way around?" he asked Alistrair.

They found the Urijah elder back to pacing again, but without agitation this time. He appeared to be giving the question considerable thought. "Considering all the unique events which occurred – a village bride with the skill of a warrior and the bravery of our founding father himself, three unattached warriors set on challenging for her hand knowing such would be impossible, forming a triad uniting two villages to claim the daughter of a third... Only the Creator could have foreseen such an outrageous outcome."

"And now your new family unit lays claim to a child from outside the borders of any village?" Enoch asked, his eyes moving toward Jemina again. She nodded and moved back to stand with her mates.

"Thank you for not calling him an evildoer, sir." She was engulfed by her men, Loinbard from behind, Anders and Aras at the sides.

"Children are innocents; it is only when one is an adult that actions cause people to feel the need to place labels on them. As chief elder of Finn, I take no pleasure in the responsibility of taking such action against two of my own people." Enoch moved so all gathered could hear his verdict. "Hendrix and Johan, you have been found guilty of attempted murder of a child from three villages."

Johan toppled his chair as he objected. "The boy is an evildoer, roaming the area outside of civilized communities. He may be young now, but think you he won't grow up to threaten those in the city and villages! Had we come upon a cougar cub like those fools did, would you expect us to bring it here so these villagers can raise it? It will grow into a wild beast and pray upon those foolish enough to let it live. It is so with the boy, too. Destroying a threat now is better than waiting for it to become more dangerous."

"Our ancestors learned the truth about evil long ago," Enoch scowled at him. "It is not born of flesh, but cultivated by malicious actions. It cannot be determined by laying eyes on a person, but from regarding his behavior. The only evildoers I see here are you two, former Finn warriors. As for the boy having no village to call home. You have none, but he now has three. His mother is from Urijah and his fathers are from Finn and Konrad."

Loinbard brushed aside Jemina's red hair so he could be better seen. "It's Konrad-Finn, sir."

SMILEY FOUND the Village of Konrad to his liking once he settled in. The village elders had welcomed Anders, son of Finn without hesitation. They had been a bit less hospitable to the ferocious looking hound at first. Jemina got him to perform a few of the tricks he had mastered as a pup. Concern for the beast waned when the villagers saw a wee bride commanding him to sit, lay, and turn over.

Soon children were begging their parents for a pet like the new Konrad-Finn bride had. Smiley was allowed to roam around the outer ring of their new home during the heat of the day, and only tethered outside at nighttime as an added level of protection against any who might try to breach their family unit.

The sheer number of new people she met had Jemina's head swimming the first few days. Most of them were family members. But she soon came to understand there was an intimate group within that set. Her new fathers-in-law, Ryder, Wolf and Kia were a secret, serious lot. They watched over their wife, Attie and young children with sharp eyes.

For her part, Attie welcomed Jemina without reservation. She promised to help the new bride learn the ways of her new home and begin transitioning to Konrad customs. "They are a serious lot," Attie had confided. "Trust is not something easily earned, but once you are accepted within the ranks, you will be privy to more secrets than you care to know."

Jemina knew Loinbard and Aras harbored some dark secret they had yet to share with her. Whatever it was, it troubled them deeply. When the time came for her to learn of it, Jemina promised she would guard it and her new husbands with her very life.

She still had not met Anders people. In the morning, he, Aras and Loinbard would travel to the village of Finn to escort his mother and younger siblings back to Konrad. Enoch would have returned home from his time at Urijah by then and had time to explain the situation to all involved. Anders agreed to let the older boys of his mother's family unit decide for themselves if they would relocate to the new village. He knew his mother would not protest the change. Now that her husbands were dead, her heart no longer lived in Finn.

Vincent, the boy Aras, Anders, Loinbard and she had claimed as their own had found a best friend in Smiley. He rarely talked to anyone but the dog, something that worried Jemina greatly. Part of her wished Enoch had sentenced Hendrix and Johan to death rather than expelling them from all civilized societies. At least then the boy would know justice had been served and the demons that had attacked him could never return.

Aras had tried to locate the rest of the boy's family as they journeyed home but had not been successful. Her lead husband had made a pledge to the child to keep searching at a later day. Vincent sadly nodded his understanding as they pressed on toward Konrad. While his small body healed, his mind still struggled to come to terms with the abuse he had been made to suffer.

Attie, her new mother-in-law had several young sons. They were a loud, bossy lot who adopted Vincent as an honorary brother. When they played, they dragged the shy child along with them. Tonight, Vincent was staying at Attie's family unit. Thursdays were to be Aras, Anders, Loinbard and Jemina's bonding night in this village. Their family unit would be assured at least one childfree night a week to enjoy their privacy. They had made love every opportunity that presented itself, but still could not manage to get enough of one another. Tonight, though, Aras had postponed more intimate matters to discuss something of great importance involving his childhood family unit, and the impact it would no doubt have on their own.

It was a serious issue. Her first husband was taut and at a loss for words. She placed her hand in his own and lent him some of her courage. "We are a family now, Aras. Nothing you can share will jeopardize our unit."

"Loinbard wanted to share this information with you before the first claiming. He felt it was the only honorable thing to do. I selfishly did not want to delay joining in the most intimate ways with you, and pushed his concerns aside. Now I realize it was unfair to both you and Anders. You should have been given a chance to understand the battle he and I face so you could make an informed decision to join in or walk away."

"Considering all the events which led to us becoming one family unit, the Creator most want us to join forces to help in whatever battle you face, brother," Anders said. He slapped Aras on the back before sitting down to hear the details.

Loinbard pulled Jemina to rest on his lap as she listened to Aras' account. "Loinbard and I had two sisters. One died at birth, along with our first mother. We were no more than ten cycles old at the time. Having already lost two fathers recently, the deaths were quite difficult for us to comprehend. Then Ryder, our only remaining parent joined Wolf and Kia's triad. They claimed Attie from the city as a bride. We did our best to challenge the new union at first, but eventually we melted into a new family unit. Attie was a bleeder. She went to our healer when it was time to give birth to her first child. Another girl was born to our family, only we never laid eyes on her."

"Did she perish during the birthing process, too?" Jemina's heart ached for the men she loved and the losses they had been forced to bear.

Loinbard took over the tale now, cradling her as if to protect her from all evil. "Our sister lived. Attie was close to death, though. Ulthia, our healer, knew of only one cure that could stop the loss of life giving blood seeping from Attie's body. Our second mother was given a choice no mother should be forced to make. She could spare her own life by trading her newborn daughter for the lifesaving remedy."

Anders had been listening quietly until now, but now joined in the conversation, seeking clarification. "Trade with whom? Like the compound in Urijah, Finn's healer's building is impossible to penetrate. It is cocooned in the village's protective borders. Various safety boundaries separate the birthing room from invaders."

"Yet babies go missing from there every cycle," Aras said, his voice bitter. "Our elders searched high and low for the blood thirsty demons responsible. They searched everywhere but the most obvious place, the birthing room itself."

"After meeting your mother, I find it impossible to believe she would exchange any child's life for her own," Jemina countered. Attie was a loving, overprotective mother. Sacrificing one of her own children would not be an option. "I know of few mothers who would do as much."

"She did not make the decision," Aras said. He began walking around the room, a nervous energy filling him. "Attie refused outright. The healer had already watched my birth father Ryder deal with the loss of one wife. She could not bear for him to do so again, so she chose a course of action that exposed the entire web of lies involving babies who go missing from the birthing rooms. Ulthia brought my father and his new triad into the room where their wife was slowly bleeding to death.

"Then the healer told them about the Tree of Life which grows in the city. One seed would bring their beloved back, but it came at a terrible cost. If they chose to save Attie, they had to forfeit their daughter to the city to receive the seed." Aras stopped pacing. His eyes came to rest on Jemina. For the first time in his life, he truly understood how his father could make such a desperate decision. A part of him had always resented

Ryder for giving up his flesh and blood child, an innocent baby. Yet now he knew the depth of love a man could have for a woman. Creator forgive him, he would do the same, desperate thing if necessary, to save his beloved Jemina.

"The city is miles away from here. How could the baby be taken from the healer's compound, past village guards and safely delivered to the wall?" Anders insisted on more details.

"There is a secret passage hidden in the birthing room. The very bed grooms and their brides seal their final claiming on, the one where wives go to deliver their babes, harbors a hidden lever. When pulled, the bed moves aside, revealing a stairwell underground. Tunnels lead to the center of the city, where another hidden opening allows the exchange of a female babe for the lifesaving fruit."

For hours, Jemina and Anders posed questions, trying to come to terms with the painful history Aras and Loinbard shared. They learned Aras' father had made another desperate deal the day he gave up their sister. The girl would be sent outside the city as a potential bride when she reached seventeen cycles. Then Aras' family planned to take her back home where she belonged. Until then, the secret had to be maintained, guarded, in hopes of seeing their sister again.

Eventually Jemina and Anders came to the same conclusion. "Then we must wait until our sister is safe to punish this injustice?" Anders said. There was never any question he would support Aras and Loinbard. They had accepted the responsibility of his own mother and blood brothers. The moment they formed a triad, their sister became his.

"No wonder you dislike healers," Jemina said, going to Aras and running her hand along his hard jaw. "I support you and any cause you face, husband."

The new family unit shared a passionate night. Each claimed her womb, planting their seed deep within, promising to protect her and any babies the Creator blessed them with. Jemina used her hands to stroke the husbands not laying between her legs. Anders suggested again another form of love making involving her lips, but Jemina had balked at the very idea. She found such an idea revolting. Husbands are meant to please their wife, not the other way around. He temporarily dropped the subject, promising to bring it up again.

IN THE MORNING, Jemina woke with a sated smile. Her husbands had departed before daybreak. She pondered everything she had learned the night before. After recalling her twin brother's wife was a bleeder from the city, she had been distraught with the need to warn Jael. At first, her husbands had been adamant about not revealing the secret and she had wept bitter tears. Then Aras had relented. He promised they would warn Jael of the danger after returning with Anders' family.

Her only resentment was their insistence she remain behind for both trips. She was a warrior, Jemina had argued, an asset to their traveling party. But they overruled her. She wondered if their second love making session had not been initiated to exhaust her so they might leave without her continuing the debate.

Inspiration struck and Jemina started making a plan of her own. While her men were off to the Village of Finn, she could easily pay a visit to the village of Urijah, warn her brother and be back before anyone was the wiser. In fact, she reasoned, doing so would probably please her mates, saving them a trip away from Konrad. She and Smiley would enlist the help of her new brothers from Aras' and Loinbard's family unit. The older boys were fledglings. They would savor a chance to explore outside the village limits. With her to guide them, they would get experience to aid them in their official training.

A nagging feeling gripped her as Jemina prepared to follow

through with her plan. Hadn't she dreamed of something similar happening? Details were hard to recall, but she did remember surviving the ordeal. Shaking her head, she steeled her determination. Jemina was off on a new adventure.

21

Retrieving their Wayward Wife

Aras knew trouble was coming when he found the Konrad healer Ulthia waiting for him at the border. Anders' mother and brothers had managed the trip between villages well, making it possible to achieve remarkable time. The three men had discussed settling the newcomers in so they might venture off to visit Jemina's brother. They knew she would likely beg to come with them, so they hoped to fill her time with helping her new in-laws find their way around the area.

"Welcome to Konrad." The healer greeted Anders' mother. "I will be happy to show you the way to your new home."

Aras studied Ulthia, realizing for the first time how old and weary she seemed. He steeled his heart against the pity he felt. Yes, at one time, this woman had helped raise him and his brothers when their father had been forced to serve another year on the city wall. They had formed a strong bond and considered her along the lines of a doting grandmother. But he could not forget her part in helping the city steal village daughters from their families. Maybe, when his sister was returned to Konrad, he would be able to release some of the resentment he harbored for

Ulthia, but not yet. "We will show Mother Gwen and her sons where they will be living."

Ulthia gave him a smile and reached in her pocket to remove a small package. "Noon is fast approaching, Aras. It is best for your triad to begin your journey to the Village of Urijah. I am sure you want to make sure your wife and blood brothers made it there without trouble."

Her words did not make any sense to him. He wondered why she was acting as if they were still on friendly terms. Of anyone coming to welcome Anders' family, the healer was the last person he would have considered. Aras was shocked his little Jem had not parked herself at the village border to wait for their return. She would probably still be mad about them leaving her behind and want to insist they take her on the trip to see her brother.

His blood brother and Anders were quicker to realize what was happening. Loinbard tensed, his voice low and deadly. "Did Jemina hound the village elders into letting her go back home for the day?"

Ulthia maintained her serene expression, but her eyes were full of concern. "I do not believe the elders realize your determined wife is even up and about. I may have given them the impression she was exhausted from all the excitement of the past few weeks and was recouping in her family unit."

"Did she leave here alone?" Aras' heart nearly seized with fear. It was dangerous to travel outside the village limits. Grown men did so only when in groups. Jemina would not be foolish enough to do something so perilous. She had too much sense.

"Your blood brothers Schuyler, Konnor and Geofrey joined her for the trip." Giving the three men a chance to consider their options, Ulthia started providing Gwen, Anders' mother with information. "Schuyler is sixteen. The fledglings' trainers are very impressed with his progress. He hopes to earn his warrior status. Unless he does something foolish, he may graduate top of his cycle. Konner is fifteen and Geofrey, just fourteen. They still have a few more years of training to go. Hopefully they don't have any setbacks, either."

Her subtle hints were not lost. Not only had Jemina left the safety of Konrad land, she somehow ended up with three young fledglings, his own younger brothers. If they managed to survive the dangerous journey, there would be hell to pay from the village elders. Leaving without permission was a punishable offense. It would carry the penalty of hot poker strikes across the back and loss of position in rank among other fledglings.

"Did you try to reason with them?" Anders demanded and the healer visibly flinched at his tone. Gwen frowned at her son, but he pushed for more facts.

The healer gave her answer to his mother. "Only one person in the village saw them leave. Aras has many younger siblings. Fox is only nine. He is constantly begging his parents and the elders to let him begin training as a fledgling. The dear child is constantly following after his older brothers and trying to learn everything he can about being a warrior. He was very disappointed when his new sister-in-law did not allow him to join the wonderful adventure she had planned. He was going to take up the issue with Otto, our head healer, when I intercepted him."

"Where is the boy now?" Loinbard demanded. Anders' younger brothers huddled around their mother's skirts. All through the walk over, the boys had idolized the youngest of the triad. He had entertained them, never scolding them when they got into mischief. The angry man before them now was frightening, indeed.

Ulthia found the courage to speak directly to Aras. "I have him guarding Smiley and Konfin, the cat. Both animals have been protesting loudly about being left behind. If you like, I could take Gwen and her sons to meet their new pets. I suggest leaving the heavier things you brought with you here. They will be safe and can be collected later."

He nodded solemnly. The healer had protected his family as

best as she could. It was now up to him and his triad to retrieve Jemina and the others before matters turned even more disastrous. Aras knew he should be thanking her, but the words would not form no matter how grateful he was. As he was preparing to turn and leave, her frail hand reached up to clasp his arm.

"You will want to take this with you." The healer handed him the small package she had been carrying. "Fox mentioned something about Jemina's sister-in-law being a bleeder. That's when I understood the urgency of your wife's decision to return home to warn her twin brother. It is important to guard the gift carefully. Only a few of these can be found outside of the city. The cost of replacing it, is something I can no longer stomach. It need not be used after every birth. Bleeding is not deadly when boys are born, only girls. They should save this gift until it is necessary to spare a life."

The small package, wrapped in brown paper and string, looked small in his large hand. It weighed next to nothing. Yet inside was the ransom for life and death. He had matched wits with the city of women to save Giannis once. His birth mother perished because she gave birth to a stillborn daughter and could not meet the demanded price. Attie, his second mother, received the seed, but only after having her daughter stolen from her arms.

He looked at the old healer. The cycles had not been kind to her. Her hair was gray. Wrinkles of worry and regret etched across her once flawless face. Given a second chance, he doubted she would agree to go along with the city's deception. She was doing what she could to atone for her sins.

Before he could harden his heart against her again, he reached down to pull her into a tight hug. She winced, and he feared he might have accidently broken one of her brittle bones. He quickly released her and inspected her back. Her dress was thin, almost sheer in some places. Aras saw the scars of line after line of burn marks along her back. From the odd angle they had been applied, he suspected she had inflicted the damage on herself.

Loinbard and Anders motioned for him to stop wasting precious time. Aras gave the healer one last look of compassion before rushing off to find their wayward bride.

JEMINA TRIED to talk to her husbands on the journey back to Konrad. Their expressions of disappointment and fury cut at her heart. From the second they found her sleeping in her parents' family unit at Urijah, they had been unable to even glance at her without frowning. She was not surprised that they had followed her here. Jemina had just had a vivid dream about them doing so. She was starting to believe her visions were more than just wishful thinking.

Had there been other dreams that foretold future events, she wondered. Jemina had lots of time to reflect on the matter during the silent walk back to Konrad. Her young brothers-in-law, who had been chattering birds the entire journey to Urijah, now would not even look her way. Her ears were still ringing from Aras' heated lecture when they were away from witnesses. The rules of Konrad were so much stricter than her birthplace. She never would have invited them to come if she knew it might cost them their positions in training. Jemina still found it hard to believe anyone would take a hot rod to the back of young boys who had merely sought to have a bit of adventure.

The three Konrad fledglings managed to slip back inside the border of Konrad without being noticed. The border guards were too busy dealing with Jemina and her husbands, who sought to return in a more noticeable way. They were hauled off to face the village elder and a long, drawn out meeting followed.

Many of the village residents had heard rumors that the new village bride had cast off her husbands and run back to Urijah to seek sanctuary. Whispers of possible wars and other nonsense reached Jemina's ear as she listened to the elders' debate. "I have not cast off my husbands!" she hissed at one redheaded woman who seemed to be trying to cause more drama. "I suggest you stop spreading lies before I come over there and make you."

Anders yanked her back when Jemina started to jerk in the redhead's direction. "Remain silent and do not move from this spot." His voice was low and did not suggest it would be wise to disobey. So she stayed still, but her eyes shot daggers in the other woman's direction.

A cluster of young boys sitting around a pretty, older woman caught Jemina's attention then. If she had any sons, she imagined they might look like these youngsters. They favored her second husband. Could the boys be his blood brothers? She might have asked had he not been so unreasonably grumpy at present. Then she recalled Anders did not grow up in this village and realized the woman was likely his mother. Their eyes locked for just a second before Jemina broke contact.

What a way to meet her new mother-in-law! The poor woman had just arrived in a new village because her son formed a strange triad to marry her. What must she think about Jemina? Could Anders' mother hear the gossipers whispers of run-away brides, possible wars, and strikes with a hot poker?

Anytime Jemina tried to address Otto, the elder in charge, her husbands ordered her to remain quiet. Deciding it was best to stay focused. She sighed with relief when Otto dismissed all charges against her husbands. They had sought approval to leave for both the villages of Finn and Urijah before departing. She was not so wise. The elders found her guilty and a surprised hush filled the meeting area.

Jemina was sentenced to three strikes of the hot rod for her violation. Recalling the brave way Aras had accepted a similar penalty, she prayed she might be able to do the same. But terror made her nauseous.

Otto removed his cloak and shirt. "... since the first man defied the village law sixty cycles ago, punishment for leaving our boundaries without approval has been set in flesh. It is my duty to carry it out now."

"You are a warrior," Jemina muttered to herself. "You will not flinch." She watched in horror as he removed a glowing staff from the burning fire.

Otto gripped the weapon with his cloak and approached her. "For leaving the village without permission, you will receive a burning reminder of what happens when anyone breaks our laws. You may choose to refuse this punishment but will be banished."

Before she could voice her decision, Anders' stepped between her and the elder. "I seek to take my wife's portion." He yanked his shirt over his head and stood on the center block. His strong, tan shoulders were wide and perfect. Not a scar marred the area.

Otto did not seem surprised by the action. "You may take her portion of the fire staff, but this requires you to use a regular staff to strike her yourself. She will still face pain, but you will be allowed to carry her scar. Punishments are public, Anders. The correction will be delivered to her backside, but your triad may block the view. Do you agree to these terms?" A silent nod was Anders only reply.

Otto swung back the fiery rod and slammed it across the younger man's skin. Anders barely flinched, and did not cry out.

The smell of singed skin filled Jemina's lungs and she cursed ever disobeying her husbands. "I will not allow anyone else to pay the price for my sins." Aras pulled her back and demanded she remain silent.

Loinbard replaced Anders then, his bare back awaiting punishment. "I seek to take my wife's portion." It shamed Jemina, and she buried her face in Aras' hard chest. She could not watch another man she loved suffer because of her actions.

The sound of the rod connecting with skin would haunt her for cycles.

Aras pulled her arms from around his neck and forced her to stand by Anders. She dared not clutch to her second husband for strength for fear of accidently increasing his pain. "Please, let me face this last strike. Your back is already scarred," she begged Aras, but he unbuttoned his shirt and stepped forward.

"I seek to take my wife's portion." Soon a second mark marred his muscular back.

When the time came, Jemina did not protest the order to move toward the center spot. She leaned forward, providing a target to accept her consequences. Otto stood close by, supervising. Anders retrieved a rod not in the fire.

"Strike with meaning, my friend. If you do not deliver a sufficient punishment, she will face the original correction in addition," Otto cautioned.

Loinbard and Aras blocked her from the others' view as Anders reached to pull down her warrior pants. The cold air made her shiver, but the feel of angry metal across her skin quickly replaced it. Each of her mates applied one stroke of the unforgiving rod across her backside. They were not overly harsh; nor were they lenient. She accepted without complaint, hoping things were finally right between them.

Jemina righted her clothes and walked from the center area without a word. She assumed her husbands were behind her, but she could not bring herself to turn back and see. The faces of all the Konrad villagers gawking shamed her in a way she had never been before. How would she be able to live here after all that had transpired? Did many of them really believe she had run away from her husbands? Could she ever really be accepted here after all which had happened?

A hand came to rest on her shoulder, but she knew it was not one of her husbands. It was too small and soft. Jemina spun around to find Aras and Loinbard's second mother, Attie. The older woman pulled her into a tight embrace before leading her to a more private place. "Do not lose heart, my new daughter. This will soon pass. I stood on that platform many cycles ago, shortly after coming to live in this village. My husbands' bear scars they accepted in my place and I had to endure a public sanction from them for all to see."

Squeezing Attie's hand, Jemina took a moment to find her voice. "In all my life in Urijah, I never heard, but less saw, anyone being sentenced in this manner. Maybe I am not suited for this village. Being an outsider was daunting enough, but now I fear the others will reject me for my stupid behavior."

"I was an outsider, too," Attie confessed. "Being a city bride, I was ignorant of so many rules and expectations observed by the Konrad people. I left the grounds to help one of my friends. Aside from the cast-off named Liora, my transgression was soon forgotten. No one ever mentioned it again. You are a brave, skilled warrior, Jemina. Few here understand how much of a challenge that puts you in as you learn our ways. But you have already etched out a place in many hearts."

"I will help." The timid voice surprised them both. They spun around to find Anders' mother standing nearby. "Of course, my help will be very limited as I will be trying to find my own way in this new home, too. When my husbands brought me to Finn for the first time, I hated village life and longed to return to the city. But my feelings for them grew deeper with each passing day, so I forced myself to adjust. My son must have a very strong connection to you, Jemina, village daughter of Urijah. He knows no other life except for Finn. I feared he might resent having to move away because of his new triad. The moment he arrived to bring me here, he assured me moving was never a concern for him. Once he fell in love with you, he knew his home would be where you were."

"It is the same with all of her husbands," Aras announced. "Come, wife. It is time for us to return to our home." Loinbard and Anders had found them. His fathers were standing close by. Aras faced Gwen. "Ma'am, I realize it is your first day in our village, but would you mind spending a few days with my mother and fathers before settling into your new home with us?"

Jemina did not want to let go of the comfort being offered by her two new mothers. Her husbands, though devoted enough to claim scars meant for her, were still disappointed in her. She wanted things to go back to normal, but was unsure of what she needed to do to bring about such an action.

22

Dreams Come to Pass

Alone in their family unit, she found herself led to the center most room. Aras told her to wait inside so the triad could discuss how to proceed. Trying to avoid fretting about what they might be thinking, she walked around straightening things. Unlike the homes in Urijah, which were built in levels, Konrad had a single floor. A larger room for the warriors gave way to an area where children bunked down. Within the circle, was the heart of the home, where the wife resided. Anders had suggested they modify the center area so his mother could have her own portion, allowing everyone more privacy. Jemina had insisted his mother could have the entire center circle as she planned to spend her nights in the outer wing with them.

She was a trained warrior, after all, the least in need of protection. She grimaced recalling her arrogance. Thinking in such a manner had led her to this very point. What was keeping her husbands? Did they know how excruciating waiting for them would be? Probably, she bit her bottom lip. Loinbard would recommend making her dwell on her transgression.

The door seal parted and Jemina jumped. Now she was

certain it was too soon to face them. Aras' eyes still showed his feeling of betrayal. Anders' stance mirrored his disappointment and Loinbard appeared ready to pounce on her unexpectedly. Anders spoke first, his voice deadly calm. "Jemina, it is important for us to understand why you did not honor our request to remain within the safety of the village today. Communication between family units is necessary if they are to build strong relationships."

She tried to swallow the lump in her throat. "Well, I… It's hard to put into words. The moment I woke up, my brain was filled with dozens of changes. I could scarcely remember the names of all the people I have met. Meeting your elders, learning about your family secrets, discussing where Anders' family might live in our new family home."

"Stop delaying," Aras demanded. He had not raised his voice, but she still flinched. "Explain why you chose to dishonor our family and dared to convince others to help you?"

His dark tone startled her. Why she wasn't terrified, Jemina could not fathom. A skilled warrior would cringe under the livid expression Aras was giving her. These proud, wonderful men would never truly cause her harm. They had sworn to protect her, not once, but twice. They carried her scars, a lifelong symbol of their devotion to her.

Anything she offered by way of explaining would be hollow to even her own ears. Yet they stood there, waiting for her to explain. "I had to tell my brother. He needs to protect his wife."

Anders' hand raked through his long hair, nearly pulling out the strap of leather holding much of it behind his head. Exhaling with frustration, he spoke, "Giannis is under no immediate danger, wife. If she is with child, it would take months for the real threat to come to pass. You are more intelligent than most. Do not try to claim you don't understand as much."

Aras and Anders started circling her and shame coursed through her very core. Recalling them doing just this when they gave their pledges to protect her, she dropped her eyes. Jemina could not bear to witness the disappointment in their eyes. "I did not realize you three would pay the price for my actions. All I could think of when I left…"

"You agreed to let us handle the task," Loinbard interrupted her as he stood watching from near the door. Was he blocking the exit or putting distance between them until he could regain control of his temper? She glanced up to see his piercing sky-blue eyes glaring at her betrayal of his trust.

"Do you deny remembering our promise to return to your village and share the secret with Jael?" Her downcast face was the only confirmation Loinbard needed. She should have waited. She would no longer try to explain her way out of whatever punishment they planned for her. Still he lectured her.

"Bride, our family has protected the confidence we shared with you for many cycles. Our sister's life depends on guarding it until she comes of age. After such a time, everyone will know of the city's deceit. No one outside of our immediate family unit can know the full story. Not even Otto, who is trusted more than any other living being among us.

"Yet we did not hesitate to expose the details to you, and, in consideration of your wishes as our wife, we promised to extend this knowledge to your brother. Do you comprehend the courage such a compromise cost my blood brother and me? Despite him living far away from our family unit, knowing one slip of his tongue could jeopardize all which we have worked so hard to protect, we agreed to your request to prepare Jael to protect his wife," Loinbard finished.

"How can I make this right?" Jemina was desperate now. She longed to go back in time and undo the damage to her husbands' trust and respect for her. Whatever they asked of her, she would do it to prove how repentant she was for disrespecting their faith.

"We have gifted you with all we have to offer, Jemina. Our

protection. Our love. Our seed." Aras' voice sounded so dejected. "You will have to find a way to repair the harm done."

How could she humble herself enough to make them see her regret? Before they wed, she had been desperate to prove her worth to them. She was a village daughter. Strong. Skilled with a sword. Worthy of their respect and trust.

"I cannot undo the damage. The wounds on your backs will remind me always of the day I dishonored our union and selfishly acted alone, instead of putting our family's interest above all others. Jael and my family unit back in Urijah were my primary focus, but I forgot, as your wife, I have a new family unit that rightfully surpasses all others."

Jemina removed her clothes, tossing them aside. Her undergarments followed. She needed to bare herself, body and soul now to prove her honest, pure shame. Her three husbands watched her closely, but she did not meet their eyes. Until she had regained their respect, proven her own, she would not do so. "You have gifted me with your protection. Each of your backs confirm your devotion. The fact that you have not cast me off as a wife, even after I dishonored our family unit, proves your love knows no bounds."

Jemina swallowed hard. She would not gag, she swore to herself. This was the only way she could think to humble herself and honor the gift of their seed. The village bride dropped to her knees and prepared to do the one thing she had managed to avoid during their many lovemaking sessions since the wedding ceremony.

Anders had tried to explain the pleasure men found in such a distasteful act. Still full of pride, she had quickly reminded them that it was their job to satisfy her, not the other way around. Her village elder had been quite certain of such matters, she had told them.

Jemina had asked her mother about such things after that encounter. It was empowering to witness the control and glory a wife had by pleasing her men so thoroughly. This was where the woman's pleasure came from, her mother had explained. Still Jemina had been sure she did not need to lower herself to such distasteful acts.

It felt strange, walking on her knees to move closer to Anders. Reaching up, she slowly unfastened his pants and reached inside. His male member was easy to free. It was already engorged. Shutting her eyes tightly, she hoped to repay some of the devotion they showed to her. "Until I earn the right to receive your seed in my womb, I will accept it this way as proof of my regret for leaving the safety of the village border."

The smell was not unpleasant. It reminded her of his strength and devotion to her. Often this husband had explored her body with his mouth, especially her most intimate parts. He was skilled with flicking his hot tongue across her nub, making it swell and go damp. He was even teaching her other husbands about the ways to drive her wild with the same attention.

Could the tip of her tongue move as expertly as his did? She allowed herself to study the end. Small bits of liquid seeped from the slit there. She could not stop herself from gagging at the thought of something so unfamiliar going into her mouth. She tried to use her hair to clean the area, but it only made more fluid appear.

As if trying to rush through a dreaded chore, she stopped thinking and started acting. The dew had a musty flavor, she noted as she flicked her tongue over the tip. Her husband tensed and a moan tore from deep in his chest. He was enjoying her efforts. Pride swelled within her heart, a renewed hope taking over. She mimicked his technique, doing her best to lick the sensitive area at a feverish pace. He pulled back, moaning about being too close to losing his seed.

Jemina then switched her attention to Aras. His member was even harder than Anders' had been. With pride and determination, she repeated her earlier action, making modifications when necessary. First, she licked the impressive length. He tasted a bit stronger than Anders, but she found herself getting used to the strange sensation and wondered what her third mate would feel and taste like when she was ready to work on him. Her tongue settled over the tip of his rod. She improved on her performance and worked diligently to prove her dedication and love.

"Oh, dear Creator above, this cannot be right." Aras' voice was husky as he gripped her hair tightly while she sucked on the moisture escaping from the tip.

Anders' voice sounded odd as he stepped forward to coax her attention back on him. "I have regained my control."

Jemina had to pull against Aras' possessive hold so she could dart her tongue at Anders' penis. Lost in the moment, she switched between both men, licking the very edge around the tips of their shafts before suckling the liquid that rewarded her efforts.

Loinbard pushed his way toward her suddenly. She witnessed him strong arm his triad aside as he freed his own penis. He guided it toward her face, the look of anticipation making Jemina's own body grow damp. She reached down to start fondling herself, but he ordered her to stop.

"You do not come until each of us do," he ordered. His bold words and stern expression almost made her explode. She eagerly accepted the tip of his member inside her mouth as he arrogantly guided it there. The pungent scent he produced thrilled her. Fisting her hair, he waited until she parted her teeth more before pushing himself deeper inside. Was she meant to let him take her in the mouth as he did in her channel? Was such a thing even possible? Jemina did gag then, but only for a moment.

Loinbard gave her a chance to recover, before beginning to ease in and out of her mouth again, shallow at first, but gaining deeper and deeper access with each thrust. Her hands reached up to brace against his thighs, as if she could try gaining a bit of control over his relentless prodding. Stop thinking, she ordered herself. Let your passion guide you.

No sooner had she taken her own advice to heart then something wanton inside her took control. She reached up and pulled his pants down completely, caressing his balls. Wild, exciting sounds erupted from his throat. Jemina forced her mouth to go slack and grabbed onto his firm ass, digging her fingers in the taut muscles there. It was not long before he was tensing.

He would unload his seed soon. Fear of him slipping too far inside her mouth suddenly did not worry her. Jemina started using her tongue to playfully push his member out as he pulled back, before dutifully sucking it back inside. She was so close to exploding now.

Loinbard had ordered her not to find her satisfaction until all three of them had done so. The order repeated itself in her mind. Jemina squeezed her legs together tightly, making sure the tingling there stayed awake and ready. Hot fluid shot in her throat, and for a moment she was unsure of how to proceed.

"Open your mouth," he commanded, as he pulled himself free. "I want to see my seed filling your hot mouth before you accept every bit of it when you swallow. Can you bring yourself to do it, Little Jem? Are you really resolved on proving your devotion to our family unit?"

She complied without delay, even pushing a bit of the moisture forward with her tongue for him to view. At his nod of approval, Jemina sat on her haunches and allowed the seed to slide down her throat, even licking her lips as if appreciative of the gift he bestowed on her.

A huge smile returned to his lips. His anger and disappointment had vanished. "My pledge to protect you was never in doubt. Now rest assured my trust has been restored, too. But be warned. If you blatantly disobey us again, it won't be your mouth which claims our seed next, but your beautiful, tight ass."

"You would beat me with another steel rod?" she asked in a sassy tone, relieved at least this husband had forgiven her.

"Not beat, little Jem. Fuck. We will take turns pumping our cocks into your tight ass."

The image he planted in her mind both terrified and intrigued her.

Celebrating the small victory of making amends with one mate was cut short, her first two husbands now demanded she accept them deep within her mouth, too. Jemina started with the first, bringing him close to spilling his seed, but stopped short of finishing him off. With a wicked grin, she turned to the second, taking him to the very edge again, only to pull away.

Then she pulled at each man's legs, drawing them to stand closer to her, one on her right and one on her left. Then Jemina tried something that never entered her thoughts before this very moment. She guided both men inside her mouth. True, she could not take either in very deep, but she quickly figured out a possible solution. Jemina used the side of her mouth as a holding place for one member, as she accepted the other's hard, powerful thrust. Then her face shifted and the other member gained full access while she pocketed the other between her teeth and jaw.

Both came with a force that sent a shudder through all three of their bodies. The volume of seed was hard to contain, and some seeped between her lips as she was freed. She took a moment to regain her composure, before pooling the combined load in the center of her mouth. Opening wide, she let them see their gift to her.

After she had consumed the last ounce, they carried her to the bed they shared in the center of their new family unit. They used their mouths and fingers to bring her to completion. For a moment, Jemina actually feared she had accidently relieved herself as her body shuddered out of control. Liquid came shooting out of her frame. Would her husbands notice? She clamped her legs together tightly, only to have them forced apart by strong hands.

To her horror, Anders used his mouth to accept the fluid. Then the other two reached over to pry her legs open wider so they could lick away any remaining specks. Aras sat beside her, pulling her head to rest on his lap. "Later tonight, we will pour our seed inside your perfect body again. Only this time, we will have two entrances to fill, wife."

"We have to wait until tonight?" she pouted before relaxing and allowing sleep to claim her. She snuggled deeper into the blankets someone had generously wrapped around her and allowed sleep to envelop her.

It had been Aras who ruined the blissful moment when he explained she would be punished with another spanking for leaving the village without their knowledge. "This one won't be public, nor with a steel rod. We have agreed it would be best to give your backside a few days to recover from the older punishment. You have a nasty habit of going places you do not belong, wife. It is our job to protect you and help you learn from your mistakes."

Everything about that night felt surreal to Jemina. Only a few days before she was a virgin, unaware wives might use their mouths to please a husband. But strangely, she felt as if she had already lived tonight before. How could that be?

Bolting up in in the bed, she remembered the dream she had on the day she and her fathers departed Urijah. Aras pulled her back down to lay between them once he checked to make sure there was no danger. Anders and Loinbard returned the weapons they had seized and reached to pat her back and lull her back to sleep.

Sleep was impossible for a long time. Jemina tried to understand how she could have dreamed about this very night in such great detail. Even the faces and personalities of her three husbands had been vivid, yet she had not even set eyes on them.

Were there other dreams she could recall? Jemina searched her mind. When she was very young, she often had wonderful dreams about the adventures of a beautiful princess escaping from the city of women.

Sighing with fond memories, she recalled the beautiful girl being carried off by brave, older warriors. She was also chased by dashing gentlemen intent on marrying her. Then she joined forces with the princess and more exciting escapades followed. They become dear friends.

A smile crept across her face; the princess and Jemina became close as blood sisters. They spent much time together, discussed life in the city and thinking up ways to free the other princesses locked behind the three walls there.

Wouldn't it be exciting if those dreams became reality, too? Maybe one day she might even meet a city princess who would become her sister.

The End

Abby Aaron

Abby Aaron reported for a small newspaper in her home parish in Louisiana. She won several Louisiana Press Associate Awards before giving up that job. She has been married for 28 years to her real-life hero. They have four children, two of whom did not join the family until Abby was forty years old. (God has a sense of humor.) Her goal is to make readers laugh and lose themselves in her stories. Follow her on Facebook or visit her website: Rubycaine.com.

Don't miss these exciting titles by Abby Aaron and Eclipse Press!

Claiming Their Bride Series
Claimed By The Village of Konrad - Book One
Claiming Their Village Bride - Book Two

Blushing Books

Blushing Books is one of the oldest eBook publishers on the web. We've been running websites that publish spanking and BDSM related romance and erotica since 1999, and we have been selling eBooks since 2003. We hope you'll check out our hundreds of offerings at http://www.blushingbooks.com.

Lightning Source UK Ltd.
Milton Keynes UK
UKHW010920310120
357948UK00001B/6